"Commander Erica Griffin reporting for duty, sir." She stood at attention and saluted.

"At ease, Commander."

Dr. Thorne Wilder turned around slowly, his body stiff, and she tried not to let out the gasp of surprise threatening to erupt from her.

Brilliant blue eyes gazed at her.

Eyes she'd seen countless times in her mind. Eyes she'd seen that night before he'd disappeared. They were hauntingly beautiful and they brought back the memory of what he'd said before she'd had to put him under for surgery…and changed his life for ever.

"You're so beautiful. Beautiful. Like an angel."

No man had ever said that to her before.

As Erica stared into Captain Wilder's blue eyes a warmth spread through her. She'd always wondered what had happened to him. Since he'd been moved against her wishes, she'd assumed he hadn't made it.

She had been wrong. The man who had begged her not to take his leg was here, in Okinawa of all places, and he was a commanding officer.

Her commanding officer.

And that meant he was totally off-limits.

Dear Reader,

Thank you for picking up a copy of *Taming Her Navy Doc*.

I have a huge admiration for the men and women who serve in the armed forces. I recently met a naval officer who said that, "To give the ultimate sacrifice to your country is why men and women *serve* their country."

His words touched me so deeply. My family has a military history, dating back to when Canada was not a country but a colony of Great Britain. My admiration for those who serve runs deep.

Thorne made the ultimate sacrifice for his country. He loved being a SEAL, and in one tragic circumstance that was all taken away from him—by the woman who has now come to the naval base he's stationed at. He's conflicted by the promise he made to his dying brother and his desire for Commander Erica Griffin. He's not sure he deserves happiness.

I hope you enjoy reading Thorne and Erica's story as much as I enjoyed writing it.

I love hearing from readers, so please drop by my website, amyruttan.com, or give me a shout on Twitter @ruttanamy

With warmest wishes

Amy Ruttan

TAMING HER NAVY DOC

BY
AMY RUTTAN

MILLS
BOON

First published in Great Britain 2015
by Mills & Boon, an imprint of Harlequin (UK) Limited,
Eton House, 18-24 Paradise Road, Richmond, Surrey, TW9 1SR

© 2015 Amy Ruttan

ISBN: 978-0-263-25843-1

Harlequin (UK) Limited's policy is to use papers that are natural,
renewable and recyclable products and made from wood grown in
sustainable forests. The logging and manufacturing processes conform
to the legal environmental regulations of the country of origin.

Printed and bound in Great Britain
by CPI Antony Rowe, Chippenham, Wiltshire

Born and raised on the outskirts of Toronto, Ontario, **Amy Ruttan** fled the big city to settle down with the country boy of her dreams. When she's not furiously typing away at her computer she's mom to three wonderful children, who have given her another job as a taxi driver.

A voracious reader, she was given her first romance novel by her grandmother, who shared her penchant for a hot romance. From that moment Amy was hooked by the magical worlds, handsome heroes and sigh-worthy romances contained in the pages, and she knew what she wanted to be when she grew up.

Life got in the way, but after the birth of her second child she decided to pursue her dream of becoming a romance author.

Amy loves to hear from readers. It makes her day, in fact. You can find out more about Amy at her website: amyruttan.com

Books by Amy Ruttan

Mills & Boon® Medical Romance™

Safe in His Hands
Melting the Ice Queen's Heart
Pregnant with the Soldier's Son
Dare She Date Again?
It Happened in Vegas

**Visit the author profile page at
millsandboon.co.uk for more titles**

This book is dedicated to all of
those men and women who give the ultimate sacrifice.
Thank you.

PROLOGUE

IT WAS PITCH-BLACK and she couldn't figure out why the lights were off at first. Erica moved quickly, trying to shake the last remnants of sleep from her brain. Not that she'd got much sleep. She'd come off a twenty-four-hour shift and had got maybe two, possibly three, hours of sleep. She wasn't sure when the banging on her berth door roused her, telling her they needed her on deck.

What struck her as odd was why had the hospital ship gone into silent running.

She'd been woken up and told nothing. Only that some injured officers were inbound. She hadn't even been told the nature of their injuries. When she came out on deck, there was only a handful of staff and a chopper primed and waiting.

Covert operation.

That was what her gut told her and the tension shared by those waiting said the same thing.

Top secret.

Then it all made sense. She'd been trained and gone through many simulations of such a situation, but in her two years on the USNV *Hope* she'd never encountered one.

Adrenaline now fueled her body. She had no idea what

was coming in, or what to expect, but she knew she had to be on her A-game.

Not that she ever wasn't on her A-game. Her two years on the *Hope* had been her best yet and she'd risen in the ranks finally to get to this moment, being trusted with a covert operation. She had no doubt that was what it was because it must be important if their mission to aid a volcanic eruption disaster zone in Indonesia was being stalled. As she glanced around at the staff standing at attention and waiting, she saw it was all senior officers on deck, except for a couple of on-duty petty officers.

"How many minutes did they say they were out, Petty Officer?" Erica had to shout over the sound of waves. It was unusually choppy on the Arabian Sea, but it was probably due to the fact that the ship was on silent running. Only the stabilizers on the sides kept USNV *Hope* from tipping over. She couldn't see Captain Dayton anywhere, but then she suspected her commanding officer was at the helm. Silent running in the middle of the Indian Ocean at night was no easy feat.

"Pardon me, Commander?" the petty officer asked.

"I asked, how many minutes out?"

"Five at the most, Commander. We're just waiting for the signal."

And as if on cue a flare went off the port side and, in the brief explosion of light, Erica could make out the faint outline of a submarine. The chopper lifted from the helipad and headed out in the direction of the flare.

"Two minutes out!" someone shouted. "Silent running, people, and need-to-know basis."

Erica's heart raced.

This was why she'd got into the Navy. This was why she wanted to serve her country. She had fought for this moment, even when she had been tormented at Annapolis about not having what it took.

Dad would've been proud.

And a lump formed in her throat as she thought of her father. Her dad, a forgotten hero. She was serving, and giving it her all helping wounded warriors, and being on the USNV *Hope* gave her that. She had earned the right to be here.

The taunts that she'd slept her way to the top, telling her she couldn't make it, hadn't deterred her. The nay-saying had strengthened her more. Even when her dad suffered with his PTSD and his wounds silently, he would still wear his uniform with pride, his head held high. He was her hero. Now she was a highly decorated commander and surgeon and it gave her pride. So she held her head up high.

The better she did, the more she achieved the shame of her one mistake being washed away. At least, that was what she liked to think, even if others thought she'd end up with PTSD like her father: unable to handle the pressures, her memory disgraced. Well, they had another think coming. She was stronger than they thought she was.

The chopper was returning, a stretcher dangling as it hovered. Erica raced forward, crouching low to keep her balance so the wind from the chopper's blades wouldn't knock her on her backside.

With help the stretcher unhooked and was lifted onto a gurney. Once they had the patient stabilized they wheeled the gurney off the deck and into triage.

It was then, in the light, she could see the officer was severely injured and, as she glanced down at him, he opened his eyes and gazed at her. His eyes were the most brilliant blue she'd ever seen.

"We're here to get you help," she said, trying to re-assure him as they wheeled him into a trauma pod. He seemed to understand what she was saying, but his gaze was locked on her, his breath labored, panting through obvious pain.

There was a file, instead of a commanding officer, and she opened it; there was no name, no rank of the patient.

Nothing. Only that he'd had gunshot wounds to the leg three days ago and now an extensive infection.

Where had they been that they couldn't get medical attention right away? That several gunshot wounds could lead to such an infection?

Dirty water. Maybe they were camped out in the sewers.

"What's your name?" she asked as she shone a light into his eyes, checking his pupillary reaction. Gauging the ABCs was the first protocol in trauma assessment.

"Classified," he said through gritted teeth. "Leg."

Erica nodded. "We'll take care of it."

As another medic hooked up a central line, Erica moved to his left leg and, as she peeled away the crude dressings, he let out a string of curses. As she looked at the mangled leg, she knew this man's days serving were over.

"We'll have to amputate; prep an OR," Erica said to a nurse.

"Yes, Commander." The nurse ran out of the trauma pod.

"What?" the man demanded. "What did you say?"

"I'm very sorry." She leaned over to meet his gaze. "Your leg is full of necrotic tissue and the infection is spreading. We have to amputate."

"Don't amputate."

"I'm sorry, but I have no choice."

"Don't take my leg. Don't you dare amputate." The threat was clear, it was meant to scare her, but she wasn't so easily swayed. Being an officer in the Navy, a predominantly male organization, had taught her quickly that she wasn't going to let any man have power over her. No man would intimidate her. Something she'd almost forgotten at her first post in Rhode Island.

"Don't ever let a man intimidate you, Erica. Chances are they're more scared of you and your abilities."

She'd forgotten those words her father had told her.

Never again.

"I'm sorry." She motioned to the anesthesiologist to sedate him and, as she did, he reached out and grabbed her arm, squeezing her tight. His eyes had a wild light.

"Don't you touch me! I won't let you."

"Stand down!" she yelled back at him.

"Don't take my leg." This time he was begging; the grip on her arm eased, but he didn't let go. "Don't take it. Let me serve my…" His words trailed off as the sedative took effect, his eyes rolling before he was unconscious.

His passionate plea tugged at her heart. She understood him, this stranger. She'd amputated limbs before and never thought twice. She had compassion, but this was something more. In the small fragment she'd shared with the unnamed SEAL, she had understood his fear and his vulnerability. It touched her deeply and she didn't want to have to take his leg and end his career.

If there'd been another way, she'd have done it. There wasn't.

The damage had been done.

If he'd gotten to her sooner, the infection would have been minor, the gunshot properly cared for.

It was the hazard of covert operations.

And her patient, whoever he was, was paying the price.

"Let's get him intubated and into the OR Stat." The words were hard for her to say, but she shook her sympathy for him from her mind and focused on the task at hand.

At least he'd have his life.

* * *

"Petty Officer, where is my patient's commanding officer?" Erica asked as she came out of the scrub room.

"Over there, Commander. He's waiting for your report." The petty officer pointed over her shoulder and Erica saw a group of uniformed men waiting.

"Thank you," Erica said as she walked toward them. *Navy SEALs.*

She knew exactly what they were, though they had no insignia to identify themselves. They were obviously highly trained because when she was in surgery she'd been able to see that someone had some basic surgical skills as they'd tried to repair the damage caused by the bullets. Also, the bullets had been removed beforehand.

If it hadn't been for the bacteria which had gotten in the wound, the repair would've sufficed.

At her approach, they saluted her and she returned it.

"How's my man?" The commanding officer asked as he stepped forward.

"He made it through surgery, but the damage caused by the infection was too extensive. The muscle tissue was necrotic and I had to amputate the left leg below the knee."

The man cursed under his breath and the others bowed their heads. "What caused the infection? Couldn't it be cleared up with antibiotics?"

"It was a vicious form of bacteria," Erica offered. "I don't know much about your mission."

"It's classified," the commanding officer said.

Erica nodded. "Well, you obviously have a good medic. The repair was crude, but stable."

"He was our medic," someone mumbled from the back, but was silenced when the commanding officer shot him a look which would make any young officer go running for the hills.

"If it hadn't been for the bacteria getting in there…

Depending on whatever your situation was, it could've been caused by many factors," Erica said, trying to take the heat off the SEAL who'd stepped out of line.

"Like?" the commanding officer asked, impatience in his voice.

"Dirty water?" Erica ventured a guess, but when she got no response from the SEALs she shook her head. "I'm sorry, unless I know the details of your mission I can't help you determine the exact cause of how your man picked up the bacteria."

The commanding officer nodded. "Understood. How soon can we move him?"

"He's in ICU. He has a high temperature and will require a long course of antibiotics as well as monitoring of his surgical wound."

"Unacceptable," the commanding officer snapped. "He needs to be moved. He can't stay here."

Erica crossed her arms. "You move him and he develops a post-op fever, he could die."

"I'm sorry, Commander. We have a mission to fulfill."

"Not with my patient, you don't."

"I'm sorry, Commander. We're under strict orders. I can give him eight hours before our transport comes." The commanding officer nodded and moved back to his group of men as they filed out of the surgical bay.

Erica shook her head.

She understood the protocols. It was a covert operation, but she didn't agree with all the regulations.

Their medic was useless. He needed medical care for quite some time and as a physician she wanted to see it through.

When that young SEAL had blurted out that the man she'd operated on was their medic, her admiration for her patient grew. He'd operated on himself, most likely without anesthetic, and probably after he'd removed the bullets from the other man they'd brought on board after him. That man didn't have the same extent of infection but, from what she'd gleaned from a scrub nurse, the gunshot wound had been a through-and-through. It hadn't even nicked an artery.

The man was being watched for a post-op fever and signs of the bacterial infection but would make a full recovery.

Her patient on the other hand had months of rehabilitation and, yes, pain.

I wish I knew his name.

It was a strange thought which crept into her head, but it was there all the same, and she wished she knew who he really was, where he was from. Was he married? And, if he was, wouldn't his wife want to know what she was in for as well?

Her patient was a mystery to her and she didn't really like mysteries.

She headed into the ICU. He was extubated, but still sedated and now cleaned up. There were several cuts and scratches on his face, but they hadn't been infiltrated by the bacteria.

Erica sighed; she hated ending the career of a fellow serviceman. She grabbed a chair and sat down by his bedside.

She had eight hours to monitor him, unless she appealed to someone higher up about keeping him here for his own good. At least until he was more stable to withstand a medical transport to the nearest base.

USNV *Hope* was a floating hospital. It was not as big as USNV *Mercy*, but just as capable of taking care of his needs while he recovered. And it wasn't only the physical wounds Erica was worried about, but also the emotional ones he'd have when he recovered.

She knew about that. There were scars she still carried.

Her patient had begged for his leg because he wanted to serve. It was admirable. Hopefully, he'd get the help he needed. The help her father hadn't had.

She reached out and squeezed his hand. "I'm sorry," she whispered.

He squeezed back and moaned. "Liam?"

Erica didn't know who Liam was but she stood so he could see her. "You're okay."

His eyes opened—those brilliant blue eyes. "What happened?"

"You had a bacterial infection. Your leg couldn't be saved."

He frowned, visibly upset, and tried to get up, but Erica held him down.

"Let me go!" He cursed a few choice words. "I told you not to take it. You lied to me. You lied to me, Liam! Why the heck did you do that? I'm not worth it. Damn it, let me out of here."

Erica reached over and hit a buzzer as she threw as much of her weight on him as possible, trying to keep him calm as a nurse ran over with a sedative.

It was then he began to cry softly and her heart wrenched.

"I'm so sorry."

"It was your life, Liam. My life… I have nothing else. You left me. We promised to stay together. I need my leg to do that."

Erica didn't know who Liam was, but she got off of him as he stopped fighting back. "I'm sorry." She took his hand once more. "I'm so very sorry."

He nodded as the drugs began to take effect. "You're so beautiful."

The words caught her off guard. "I'm sorry?"

"Beautiful. Like an angel." And then he said no more as he drifted off to sleep.

Erica sighed again and left his bedside. She had to keep this man here. He couldn't go off with his unit.

He needed to recuperate, to get used to the idea that his leg was gone and understand why. He was a medic; he'd understand when he was lucid and she could explain medically why she'd taken his leg.

Pain made people think irrationally. She was sure that was why her father had gone AWOL during a covert mission, endangering everyone. That was why he had come home broken and that was why he'd eventually taken his own life.

"Watch out, she's going to go AWOL like her father!"

The taunts and jeers made her stomach twist.

Block them out. Block them out.

"You need to get some sleep, Commander Griffin. You've been up for over thirty hours," Nurse Regina said as she wrote the dosage in the patient's chart. "Seriously, you look terrible."

Erica rolled her eyes at her friend and bunk mate before yawning. "Yeah, I think you're right. Do you know where Captain Dayton is?"

"He's in surgery now the ship isn't on silent running," Regina remarked. "Is it urgent?"

"Yeah, when he's out could you send him to my berth? I need to discuss this patient's file with him."

"Of course, Commander Griffin."

Erica nodded and headed off to find her bunk.

She was going to fight that man's unit to keep him on the hospital ship so he could get the help he needed.

There was no way any covert operation was going to get around her orders. Not this time. Not when this man's life was on the line.

He deserved all the help she could give him.

The man had lost a leg in service to his country. It would take both physical and mental healing.

He'd paid his price and Erica was damn well going to make sure he was taken care of.

CHAPTER ONE

Five years later, Okinawa Prefecture, Japan

"CAPTAIN WILDER WILL see you now, Commander Griffin."

Erica stood and straightened her dress uniform. She'd only landed in Okinawa five hours ago on a Navy transport and she was still suffering from jet lag. She'd flown from San Diego after getting her reassignment from the USNV *Hope* to a naval base hospital.

Another step in her career she was looking forward to, and the fact that it was in Japan had her extremely excited.

It was another amazing opportunity and one she planned to make the most of. Hopefully soon she'd get a promotion in rank but, given her track record, it seemed like she had to fight for every promotion or commendation she deserved.

It's worth it. Each fight just proves you can do it. You're strong.

Captain Dayton taking a disgraced young medical officer under his wing and letting her serve for seven years on the *Hope* was helping her put the past to rest.

Helping her forget her foolish mistake, her one dumb moment of weakness.

Erica followed the secretary into the office.

Dr. Thorne Wilder was the commanding officer of the

general surgery wing of the naval hospital. They wouldn't see as much action as they'd see in a field hospital, or on a medical ship, but she'd be caring for the needs of everyone on base.

Appendectomies, gall bladder removals, colectomies—whatever needed to be done, Erica was going to rise to the challenge.

Dr. Wilder had requested her specifically when she'd put in for reassignment to a Naval hospital. She'd expected some downtime in San Diego while she waited, but that hadn't happened and she didn't mind in the least. She'd spent almost a year after her disgrace at Rhode Island in San Diego, waiting to be reassigned, and then she'd been assigned to the *Hope*. Perhaps her past was indeed just that now.

Past.

It also meant she didn't have to find temporary lodging or, in the worst-case scenario, stay with her mother in Arizona where Erica would constantly be lectured about being in the Navy. Her mother didn't exactly agree with Erica's career choice.

"You're in too much danger! The Navy killed your father."

No, the Navy hadn't killed her father. Undiagnosed PTSD had killed her father eventually, even if his physicians had had a bit of a hand in it by clearing him to serve in a covert mission.

Her mother wanted to know why she hadn't gone in to psychiatry, helped wounded warriors as a civilian. Though that had been her intention, working in an OR gave her a sense of satisfaction. Being a surgeon let her be on the front line, to see action if needs be, just like her father. It was why she'd become a medic, to save men and women like her father, both in the field and in recuperation.

"Commander Erica Griffin reporting for duty, sir." She stood at attention and saluted.

Dr. Wilder had his back to her; he was staring out the window, his hands clasped behind his back. It was a bit of an uneven stance, but there was something about him: something tugging at the corner of her mind; something she couldn't quite put her finger on. It was like when you had a thought on the tip of your tongue but, before the words could form, you lost it, though the mysterious thought remained in your head, forgotten but not wholly.

"At ease, Commander." He turned around slowly, his body stiff, and she tried not to let out the gasp of surprise threatening to erupt from her.

Brilliant blue eyes gazed at her.

Eyes she'd seen countless times in her mind. They were hauntingly beautiful.

"You're so beautiful... Beautiful. Like an angel."

No man had ever said that to her before. Of course, he'd been drugged and out of his mind with shock, but still no one had said that to her. Not even Captain Seaton, her first commanding officer when she'd been a lowly and stupid lieutenant fresh out of Annapolis. Captain Seaton had wooed her, seduced her and then almost destroyed her career by claiming she was mentally unstable and obsessed with him after she'd ended the relationship.

She was far from unstable. She had a quick temper, but over time she'd learned to keep that in check. Her job and her status in the Navy intimidated men, usually.

So his words, his face, had stuck with her. As had the stigma and that was why she'd never date another officer. She wouldn't let another person destroy her career.

Dating, if she had time, was always with a civilian. Though she didn't know why at this moment she was thinking about dating.

"Like an angel..."

As Erica stared into Captain Wilder's blue eyes, a warmth spread through her. She'd always wondered what had happened to him. Since he'd been moved against her wishes, she'd assumed he hadn't made it.

She'd apparently been wrong. Which was good.

Five years ago when she'd woken up, she realized she'd slept for eight hours. So she'd run to find Captain Dayton, only to be told that, yes, her request had been heard, but had been denied by those higher up the chain of command. When she'd gone to check on her patient, he was gone.

All traces of him were gone.

It was like the covert operation had never happened.

Those men had never been on board.

Even her patient's chart had gone; wiped clean like he'd never existed. She'd been furious, but there was nothing she could do. She was powerless, but she always wondered what had happened to that unnamed medic.

The man who had begged her not to take his leg.

The man who'd cried in her arms as the realization had overcome him.

Now, here he was. In Okinawa of all places, and he was a commanding officer.

Her commanding officer.

Dr. Thorne Wilder.

Captain Wilder.

She'd never pictured him to be a Thorne, but then again Thorne was such an unusual name and she wasn't sure many people would look at someone and say, "Hey, that guy looks like a Thorne." His head had been clean shaven when he'd been her patient, but his dark hair had grown out. It suited him.

The scars weren't as visible because he wasn't as thin, his cheeks weren't hollow, like they'd been when she'd treated him and his skin was no longer pale and jaundiced from blood loss and bacterial infection. She hadn't realized how tall he actually was—of course when she'd seen him he'd been on a stretcher. She was five foot ten and he was at least three inches taller than her, with broad shoulders.

He looked robust. Healthy and absolutely handsome.

She couldn't remember the last time she'd seen such an attractive man. Not that she'd had much time to date or even look at a member of the opposite sex.

Get a grip on yourself.

He cocked his head to the side, a confused expression on his face. "Commander Griffin, are you quite all right?"

He didn't remember her.

Which saddened her, but also made her feel relieved just the same. Erica didn't want him blaming her for taking his leg or accusing her of something which would erase all the work she'd done over the years to bring honor back to her name and shake the venomous words of Captain Seaton.

It was the pain medication. The fever. It's hardly surprising that he doesn't remember you.

"I'm fine... Sorry, Captain Wilder. I haven't had a chance to readjust since arriving in Okinawa. I'm still operating on San Diego time."

He smiled and nodded. "Of course, my apologies for making you report here so soon after you landed at the base. Won't you have a seat?" He motioned to a chair on the opposite side of his desk.

Erica removed her hat and tucked it under her arm before sitting down. She was relieved to sit because her knees had started to knock together, either from fatigue or shock, she wasn't quite sure which. Either way, she was grateful.

Thorne sat down on the other side of the desk and opened her personnel file. "I have to say, Commander, I was quite impressed with your service record. You were the third in your class at Annapolis."

"Yes," she responded. She didn't like to talk about Annapolis—because it led to questions about her first posting under Captain Seaton. She didn't like to relive her time there, so when commanding officers talked about her achievements she kept her answers short and to the point.

There was no need to delve in any further. Everything was in her personnel file. Even when she'd been turned down for a commendation because she was "mentally unfit".

Don't think about it.

"And you served on the USNV *Hope* for the last seven years?"

"Yes."

He nodded. "Well, we run a pretty tight ship here in Okinawa. We serve not only members of the armed forces and their families but also residents of Ginowan."

"I look forward to serving, Captain."

Thorne leaned back in his chair, his gaze piercing her as if he could read her mind. It was unnerving. It was like he could see right through to her very core and she wasn't sure how she felt about that.

Everyone she'd let in so far had hurt her.

Even her own mother, with her pointed barbs about Erica's career choice and how serving in the Navy had killed her father. Her mother had never supported her.

"The Navy ruined our life, Erica. Why do you want to go to Annapolis?" Erica hadn't been able to tell her mother that it was because of her father. Her mother didn't think much about him, but to Erica he was a hero and she'd wanted to follow in his footsteps.

"I'm proud to serve my country, Erica. It's the ultimate sacrifice. I'm honored to do it. Never forget I felt this way, even if you hear different."

So every remark about the armed forces ruining their life hurt. It was like a slap in the face each time and she'd gone numb with her mother, and then Captain Seaton, who had used her. She shut down emotionally to people. It was for the best.

At least, she thought she had, until a certain Navy SEAL had crossed her path five years before. He'd been the only one to stir any kind of real emotion in her in a long time.

"I have no doubt you'll do well here, Commander. Have you been shown to your quarters on base?"

"Yes."

"Are they adequate?"

"Of course, Captain."

He nodded. "Good. Well, get some sleep. Try to adjust to Okinawa time. Jet lag can be horrible. I'll expect you to report for duty tomorrow at zero four hundred hours."

Erica stood as he did and saluted him. "Thank you, Captain."

"You're dismissed, Commander."

She nodded and placed her hat back on her head before turning and heading out of the office as fast as she could.

Once she was a safe distance away she took a moment to pause and take a deep breath. She'd never expected to run into him again.

Given the state he'd been in when she'd last seen him, she'd had her doubts that he would survive, but he had and he was still serving.

Even though he was no longer a Navy SEAL, at least he hadn't been honorably discharged. It had been one of his pleas when she'd told him about his leg.

"This is your life, Liam. My life... I have nothing else. I need my leg to do that."

The memory caused a shiver to run down her spine. It was so clear, like it had happened yesterday, and she couldn't help but wonder again who Liam was. Whoever he was, it affected Captain Wilder.

It doesn't matter. You're here to do your job.

Erica sighed and then composed herself.

She was here to be a surgeon for the Navy.

That was all.

Nothing more. Dr. Thorne Wilder's personal life was of no concern to her, just like her personal life, or lack thereof, was no one else's concern.

Still, at least she knew what had happened to her stranger.

At least he was alive and that gave her closure to something that had been bothering her for five years. At last she could put that experience to rest and she could move on with her life.

After Erica left, Thorne got up and wandered back over to his window. From his vantage point he could see the walkway from his office and maybe catch a glimpse of Erica before her ride came to take her back to her quarters on base.

She'd been surprised to see him, though she'd tried not to show it. She hid her emotions well, kept them in check like any good officer.

Erica remembered him, but how much else did she remember?

Bits and pieces of his time on the USNV *Hope* were foggy to him, but there were two things he remembered about his short time on the ship and those two things were losing his leg and seeing her face.

He remembered her face clearly. It had been so calm in the tempestuous strands of memory of that time. He remembered pain.

Oh, yes. He'd never forget the pain. He still felt it from

time to time. "Phantom limb" pain. It drove him berserk, but he had ways of dealing with it.

At night, though, when he closed his eyes and that moment came back to him in his nightmares, her face was the balm to soothe him.

A nameless, angelic face tied with a painful moment. It was cruel. To remember her meant he had to relive that moment over and over again.

And then, as fate would have it, a stack of personnel files had been piled on his desk about a month ago and he'd been told to find another general surgeon to come to Okinawa. Her file had been on the top as the most qualified.

It was then he'd had a name for his angel.

Erica.

As he thought about her name, she came into view, walking quickly toward an SUV which was pulling up. He thought he adequately remembered her beauty, but his painful haze of jangled memories didn't do her justice.

Her hair wasn't white-blond, it was more honey colored. Her skin was pale and her lips red. Her eyes were dark, like dark chocolate. She was tall and even taller in her heels. He was certain she could almost look him in the eye.

She walked with purpose, her head held high. He liked that about her. Mick, his old commanding officer in the Navy SEALs Special Ops, had told him a month after his amputation that the surgeon who'd removed his leg wouldn't back down. Even when Mick had tried to scare her off.

He'd been told how his surgeon had fought for him to get the best medical care he needed. How she'd sat at his bedside. She'd seen him at his most vulnerable. Something he didn't like people to see.

Vulnerability, emotion, was for the weak.

He'd been trained to be tough.

He'd been in Special Ops for years, even though he'd started his career just as a naval medic like Erica.

And then on a failed mission in the Middle East they'd become cornered. He'd thrown himself in front of a barrage of bullets to save Tyler from being killed. Bullets had ripped through his left calf, but he'd managed to stop the bleeding, repair the damage and move on.

Only they'd been surrounded and they'd had to resort to the old sewer system running under the city to make their escape and meet their transport.

The infested and dirty water was where he'd probably caught the bacteria which had cost him his leg, but it was his leg or his life.

For a long time after the fact, he'd wanted to die because he couldn't be a Navy SEAL any longer. He'd almost died. Just like his twin brother, Liam, had on a different mission. He remembered the look of anguish on Liam's wife's face when he'd had to tell her that her husband was gone. It was why Thorne wouldn't date. Seeing the pain in Megan's eyes, the grief which ate at her and her two kids… It was something Thorne never wanted to put anyone through. It was best Thorne severed all ties. He wasn't going to stop serving and it was better if he didn't leave behind a family.

And it was his fault Liam was dead and that Megan was a widow. One stupid wrong move, that was what Thorne had done, and Liam had pushed him out of the way.

Liam had paid with his life and Thorne would forever make penance for that mistake.

Thorne had enlisted in the Special Ops and was accepted as a SEAL. It had been Liam's passion and Thorne planned to fulfill it for him.

And then he'd lost his leg saving another.

He didn't regret it.

Though he was ashamed he was no longer in the Special Ops. When he'd taken that bullet for Tyler he'd been able to see Liam's face, disappointed over another foolish move.

Thorne had returned to serve as a medic ashamed and numb to life.

He wasn't the same man anymore, and it wasn't just the absence of his leg which made him different.

At least he still had surgery. When the assignment to command the general surgery clinic in Okinawa had come up, Thorne had jumped at it—and when he'd seen that Erica, a highly recommended and decorated surgeon in the Navy, was requesting reassignment to Okinawa Prefecture, Thorne had wanted the chance to know more about the woman who'd taken his leg and saved his life.

Had she?

His mother didn't like the fact he'd gone back to serving after he lost his leg.

"I lost your brother and almost lost you. Take the discharge and come home!"

Except Thorne couldn't. Serving in the Navy was his life. He might not be an active SEAL any longer, but he was still a surgeon. He was useful.

He was needed. If he couldn't be a SEAL and serve that way, in honor of his brother he could do this.

Thorne scrubbed his hand over his face. His leg was bothering him and soon he'd head back to his quarters on the base and take off his prosthetic. Maybe soak his stump in the ocean to ease the pain. He couldn't swim, but he could wade.

Water soothed Thorne and aided him with his phantom limb syndrome. Seeing Erica face-to-face had made his leg twinge. As if it knew and remembered she'd been the one to do the surgery and was reacting to her.

Perhaps bringing her here was a bad idea.

She knew and had seen too much of his softer side. He'd been exposed to her, lying naked on her surgical table, and Thorne was having a hard time trying to process that.

Perhaps he should've kept her away.

A flash behind him made him turn and he could see dark clouds rolling in from the east. It was typhoon season in Okinawa, but this was just a regular storm. The tall palm trees along the beach in the distance began to sway as the waves crashed against the white sand.

A dip was definitely out of the question now.

The storm rolling in outside reflected how he felt on the inside and he couldn't help but wonder if he was losing his mind by bringing her here.

When had he become so morbid and self-obsessed?

He couldn't reassign her without any just cause. It would damage her reputation and he wouldn't do that to Erica.

No, instead he'd force her to ask for a reassignment on her own terms.

Though he didn't want to do it, he was going to make Erica's life here in Okinawa hard so that she'd put in for the first transfer to San Diego and he could forget about her.

Once and for all.

CHAPTER TWO

"YOU'VE BEEN HERE a week and you've been getting some seriously crummy shifts."

Erica glanced up from her charting at Bunny Hamasaki, a nurse and translator for the hospital. A lot of the residents of Ginowan knew English, but some of the older residents didn't. Bunny was middle-aged, born and bred on Okinawa. Her father was a Marine and her mother a daughter of a fisherman.

She'd been born at the old hospital down the road and seemed to know everyone and everything about everyone.

"I could say the same for you," Erica remarked.

Bunny snorted. "I'm used to these shifts. This time of night is when I'm needed the most. Plus I can avoid my husband's snoring and bad breath, working the night shift."

Erica chuckled and turned back to her charting.

Bunny reminded her of her scrub nurse, bunk mate and best friend Regina. Truth be told, she was a wee bit homesick for the *Hope* and for her friends.

This is what you wanted. You'll make captain faster this way.

And that was what really mattered—proving herself.

"I don't think I'm getting crummy shifts."

Bunny snorted again. "Commander, with all due respect, you're getting played with."

Bunny moved away from the nursing station to check on a patient and, as Erica glanced around the recovery room, she had to agree.

Since her arrival a week ago all she'd been getting was night shifts.

Which seriously sucked, because by the time she'd clocked out she was too exhausted to explore, socialize or make friends in Okinawa. Then again, she was here to work, not to make friends. After her shift, she'd return to her housing on base and collapse.

Maybe she'd unpack. Though she didn't usually do that until she'd been on-site for at least a month.

No. She'd probably just crash and sleep the day away. Except for the first day she'd arrived and met with Dr. Wilder, she hadn't seen Okinawa in the daylight.

He's putting you through your paces.

That was something she was familiar with.

Even though she was a high-ranking officer, she was positive the other surgeons were having fun initiating her, seeing how their commanding officer was doing it.

"Stupid ritual," she mumbled to herself.

"What was that, Commander?"

Erica snapped the chart closed and stood to attention when she realized Dr. Wilder was standing behind her. "Nothing, sir."

Thorne cocked an eyebrow, a smile of bemusement on his face. "You're not up for formal inspection, Commander. At ease."

Erica opened her chart again and flipped to the page she'd left off at, trying to ignore the fact that Dr. Wilder was standing in front of her. She could feel his gaze on her.

"I heard the whole conversation with Bunny," he mentioned casually.

"Oh, yes?" Erica didn't look up.

"I'm scheduling you for the night shift deliberately. You do realize that?"

"I know, Captain Wilder."

"You know?" There was a hint of confusion in his voice.

Erica sighed; she was never going to finish this chart at this rate. She set down her pen and glanced up at him. "Yes. Of course you are. I'm not a stranger to this treatment."

"I bet you're not." He leaned against the counter. "You think it's a stupid ritual?"

"I do." She wasn't going to sugarcoat anything. She never did.

His eyes widened, surprised. "Why?"

"It's bullying."

"You think I'm bullying you?" he asked.

"Of course. I'm new."

"And it doesn't bother you?"

"The ritual bothers me. I think it's not needed, but it's not going to dissuade me from my job."

There was a brief flash of disappointment. Like he'd been trying to get her to snap or something. She was made of stronger mettle than that and he'd have to do a damn lot more to sway her. She was here to stay for the long haul, or at least until she made captain—and then the possibilities would be endless.

"Well, then, you won't mind working the night shift again next week."

So much for unpacking.

"Of course not." She shrugged. "Is that all you wanted to talk about, my shift work?"

His gaze narrowed. "You're very flippant to your commanding officer."

She wanted to retort something about him being on

her operating table five years ago, but she bit her tongue. The last time she'd lost her cool, when she'd forgotten about the delicate and precise hierarchy, she'd lost her commendation. Of course, that had been a totally different situation with a former lover. Captain Wilder wasn't her lover. He was just a former patient and now her commanding officer.

She was used to this macho behavior. Erica could take whatever he had to throw at her. As long as he didn't bring up what happened during her first post, but she seriously doubted he knew all the details about it because he would've mentioned it by now.

Everyone always did.

"Sorry, sir." Though she wasn't. Not in the least.

"It won't last forever." He was smirking again.

"Can I be frank, Captain Wilder?"

He shrugged. "By all means."

"Perhaps we should go somewhere privately to discuss this."

"I don't think so."

"Fine, suit yourself." The recovery area was usually quiet, but it was even more so now, and it felt like everyone was fixated on her and Captain Wilder. "If this is your way to try and make me crack, you won't succeed."

Thorne crossed his arms. "Really? You think this is a means to drive you away?"

"I do and you won't succeed. If there's one thing you'll learn from my file, Captain, it is that I don't give up. I won't give up. So I'll take whatever you have for me, Captain, and I won't complain. So, if you're looking to see me break, you won't. If night shifts are what you want to give me, so be it. I've done countless night shifts before. It's fine. If your plan is to ostracize me, well, then, you won't succeed unless I'm the only one working and there are no patients. I'm tougher than I appear, Captain Wilder."

* * *

Thorne was impressed. He didn't want to be, but he was. She barely saw the light of day, yet she came in and did everything without a complaint. When he'd heard her mumble something about stupidity, he'd been planning to swoop in and make his kill. Push her to the breaking point.

Only she'd risen to the challenge and basically told him to bring it on.

Yes, his goal with the numerous night shifts was to ostracize her, but it wasn't working. He admired that. He didn't want to, but he did. She was right. It wouldn't work unless she was working by herself out in the middle of a desert somewhere. He was so impressed.

So she'll take whatever I give her.

It was time to throw her off.

"Tell you what. You're on days as of Saturday. Take tomorrow off and readjust your inner clock. I'll see you at zero nine hundred hours. Get some sleep. You obviously need it."

He didn't give her a chance to respond; he turned and walked away, trying not to let her see his limp, because his leg had been bothering him today, and maybe because of that he'd decided to be a bit soft on her.

No, that wasn't it. At least, that was what he told himself.

Just as she wouldn't back down, he wouldn't either.

Thorne would make sure she left the hospital and that it would be her idea. Even though he kept his distance he was always aware of what she was doing and when he was around her he felt his resolve soften because she impressed him so.

He was drawn to her.

No woman had affected him like this in a long time. Even then he wasn't sure any woman had had this kind of hold on him.

Don't think about her that way.

Only he couldn't help himself. He'd been thinking about her, seeing her face for years.

She haunted him.

Why did I bring her here?

Because he was a masochist. He was taunting himself with something, someone he couldn't have.

A twinge of pain racked through him. He needed to seek the solace of his office, so no one saw him suffer.

Erica had to go before things got out of hand.

He pushed the elevator button and when it opened he walked in. Thankfully it was empty at this time of night and he could lean against the wall and take some weight off his stump. Even if it was just a moment, he'd take it.

He waited until the doors were almost shut before relaxing, but just as the doors were about to close, they opened and Erica stepped onto the elevator.

Damn it.

He braced himself. "Can I help you, Commander?"

"Excuse me, Captain, but I don't understand why you've suddenly changed your mind about my shifts. Didn't you understand what I was saying to you?"

"I do understand English," he snapped.

Go away.

"Why did you suddenly change my shift? Especially so publically. Others will think you're being easy on me or that I'm a whiner."

"Weren't you whining?"

"No. I don't whine. You don't have to give me a day shift."

"I thought that's what you wanted."

Erica pushed the emergency stop and the elevator grinded to a halt. "I want you to treat me like any other surgeon, like any other officer. I'm not green behind the ears, or however that saying goes."

"It's *wet* behind the ears," Thorne corrected her.

"Well, I'm not that."

No. You're not.

Thorne resisted the urge to smile and he resisted the urge to pull her in his arms and kiss her. Her brown eyes were dark with what he was sure was barely controlled rage, her cheeks flushed red. She was ticked off and he loved the fire in her.

His desire for Erica was unwelcome. He couldn't have a romantic attachment.

I don't deserve it.

Emotions were weakness.

Compassion for his patients, he had that in plenty, but these kinds of feelings were unwelcome. Still, he couldn't stop them from coming, and as she stood in the elevator berating him he fought with every fiber of his being not to press her up against the elevator wall and show her exactly what he was thinking, that he'd fantasized about her for five years.

"Well?" she demanded and he realized he hadn't been listening to a word she'd been saying. He'd totally zoned out, which was unlike him. He rarely lost focus, because if you lost focus you were dead.

At least that was what he'd picked up in his years in the Navy SEALs Special Ops and on the numerous dive missions.

Tyler had lost focus and that was why the sniper would have finished him off, if Thorne hadn't thrown himself in the path. Just like the stupid mistake he'd made when Liam had thrown him out of the way and paid with his life. Thorne had only lost a leg saving Tyler's life.

Just thinking about that moment made his phantom limb send an electric jolt of pain up through his body and he winced.

"Are you all right?" Erica asked, and she reached out and touched his shoulder.

He brushed her hand away. "I'm fine." He took a deep breath.

"You look like you're in pain."

"I said I was fine!" He straightened up, putting all his weight on his prosthetic and working through the pain. "I won't give you an easy ride, but I also won't be so cruel. I realize that my actions are detrimental to your mental health."

The words "mental health" struck a chord with her. He could tell by the way the blood drained from her face. He knew they would hurt. In her file he'd read that her first commendation had been turned down due to her being unfit emotionally. Though he didn't have the details as to why, that was unimportant. His barb worked and he regretted it.

"My mental health is fine," she said quietly.

"Is it?"

She didn't glance at him as she slapped the emergency button, the elevator starting again. The elevator stopped on the next floor and the doors opened. She stepped out. The confidence, the strength which had been with her only a moment ago, had vanished.

And, though he should be pleased that he'd got to her, he wasn't. Thorne hated himself for doing that to her.

It's for the best. She's dangerous to you.

"Thank you for your time, Captain. I will see you on Saturday at zero nine hundred hours." The doors closed and she was gone and Thorne was left with a bitter taste in his mouth. His small victory wasn't so sweet.

CHAPTER THREE

"AHA!" ERICA PULLED out her sneakers from the box. "It's been a long time."

Great. You're talking to sneakers now.

Maybe she was overtired. As she glanced around the room at all the boxes she realized how disorganized her life had become.

It wasn't many boxes, but she didn't really like living in a state of chaos. She'd gone from the USNV *Hope* to San Diego and within forty-eight hours she'd been posted to Okinawa.

If she kept busy she didn't notice it so much, but now that she had some free time it irked her.

She'd rather be busy than not. Relaxation was all well and good, but she had a job to do. She stared at her bright-blue sneakers with the neon yellow laces. Although she loved running, it was not what she wanted to be doing today.

Erica would rather be in the hospital removing a gall bladder. She'd even take paperwork.

This was a new posting and she had a lot to prove.

Not only to herself, but to her comrades.

Damn Captain Wilder.

Questioning her mental health like that. How dared he?

Are you surprised?

He was probably just like Captain Seaton—threatened by her. She cursed Captain Seaton for being a major *puenez*, or "stinkbug", as her *mamère* often said about men who were scared of strong women. She was also mad at herself for being duped by Captain Seaton and letting him affect her career.

And then she chuckled to herself for condemning her superior who had given her the day off. Most people wouldn't be complaining about that and she found it humorous that she was condemning the man again.

Hadn't she done enough damage when she'd had to take his leg after it had got infected?

The guilt about ending his career as a SEAL ate at her, but not her decision to take his leg. There was no help for that. He would've died.

Perhaps he would've preferred death?

"Your father wanted to die and the Navy gave him the means to do so."

Erica shuddered, thinking about her mother's vitriol, because it made her think of that last moment she'd seen her father—the haunted look in his eyes as he'd shipped out.

"Be good, Erica. You're my girl."

He'd held her tight, but it hadn't been the same embrace she'd been used to. Three days later, he'd gone AWOL. Two weeks later, after a dishonorable discharge, he'd ended his life.

You did right by Thorne. Just like the surgeons saved your father's life the first time he was injured. You saved Thorne's life.

It was her job to save lives, not end them. His desire to die was not her concern any more. She'd saved his life and they'd taken him away. Captain Thorne Wilder was no longer her concern.

She'd done her duty by him and that was how she slept at night.

Erica sat down on her couch and slipped on her running shoes, lacing them up. There wasn't much she could do. She wasn't on duty today, unless there was an emergency, so she might as well make the best of it. Besides, running along a beach might be more challenging than running laps on a deck.

She stretched and headed out to a small tract of beach near her quarters. Though the sky was a bit dark, the sea wasn't rough, and the waves washing up on shore would make her feel like she was out on the open sea. Back on the *Hope*.

As she jogged out toward the beach she got to see more of the base. It was pretty active for being on such a small island far off the mainland of Japan.

The hospital was certainly more active than being on the *Hope*. Unless they were responding to a disaster, there were stretches at sea where they weren't utilizing their medical skills. Those stretches were filled with rigorous drills and simulations.

As she headed out onto the beach, she followed what appeared to be a well-worn path along the edge so she wouldn't have to run in the sand.

Erica opted to go off the path and headed out onto the sand. It slowed her down, but she didn't care. It would work her muscles more.

Besides, even though it was a bit overcast, it was still a beautiful day on the beach. The palm trees were swaying and the waves lapping against the shore made her smile.

As she rounded the bend to a small cove, she realized she wasn't the only one who was on the beach at this moment and it made her stop in her tracks.

Thorne.

He was about fifteen feet away from her, in casual

clothes, his arms crossed and his gaze locked on the water. She followed where he was looking and could see swimmers not too far out in the protected cove.

I have to get out of here.

She turned to leave but, as if sensing someone was watching him, his gaze turned to her. Even from a distance she could feel his stare piercing through her protective walls. A stare which would make any lesser man or woman cringe from its hard edge, but not her.

Of course, now she couldn't turn and leave. He'd seen her, there was no denying that. He walked toward her fluidly as if there was no prosthesis there. So different from yesterday when he'd moved stiffly, his chiseled face awash with pain.

His face was expressionless, controlled and devoid of emotion.

So unlike the first time she'd met him, when he'd begged her not to take his leg and made her heart melt for him just a little bit.

"Commander, what a surprise to find you here," he said pleasantly, but she could detect the undertone of mistrust. He was questioning why and she had the distinct feeling her appearance was an unwelcome one.

"It's my day off and I thought a run along the beach would be nice."

It was nice until I ran into you.

"Never heard someone mention a run as nice." He raised an eyebrow.

Erica gritted her teeth. "I haven't seen much of the base since I first arrived. I'm usually sleeping when the sun is out."

Ha ha! Take that.

He nodded, but those blue eyes still held her, keeping her grounded to the spot as he assessed her. No wonder he'd been a Navy SEAL; apparently he could read people, make them uneasy and do it all with a cold, calculating calm. Even though it annoyed Erica greatly that it was directed at her at this moment, she couldn't help but admire that quality.

It was why it made the SEALs the best of the best.

Only, she wasn't some insurgent being interrogated or some new recruit. There was a reason she'd been one of the top students in her class at Annapolis.

She wasn't weak. She was tough and stalwart and could take whatever was dished out. She'd told him as much.

This she could handle. It didn't unnerve her. When he'd shown that moment of weakness, begging for his leg, that had shaken her resolve.

"No," he finally said, breaking the tension. "I suppose you haven't seen much of the base."

Erica nodded. "No, I haven't, but I'm not complaining."

A smile broke across his face, his expression softened. "I know you're not."

"What's going on out there?" she asked.

"SEAL training," he said and then shifted his weight, wincing.

"I didn't know this base was equipped for that."

"Yes. It's where I did my training." He cleared his throat. "I mean…"

"I knew you were a SEAL." She held her breath.

He feigned surprise. Captain Wilder might be good at interrogating and striking fear into subordinates, but he wasn't much of an actor. "How?"

Erica wanted to tell him it was because she'd been the one who'd operated on him—that he'd been on her ship—only she didn't think that would go over too well. He was obviously hiding from her that he had a prosthesis, as if such a thing would make her think differently of him.

Did he think it was a sign of weakness? If he did, he was foolish, because Erica saw it as a sign of strength. A testament to his sacrifice for his country. Only she kept that thought to herself. She doubted he'd be overly receptive to it right now. The last thing she needed was to tick him off and have him state she was mentally unstable or something.

So instead she lied. "I looked up your record before I shipped out. I wanted to know who my commanding officer was in Okinawa."

His gaze narrowed; he didn't believe her. She could tell by the way he held himself, the way his brow furrowed. Only he wasn't going to admit it. "Is that so?"

"How else would I know?" she countered.

"Of course, that would be the only way you'd know." Thorne crossed his arms and turned back to look at the ocean. "Aren't you going to ask me why I'm not out there swimming with them?"

"No," Erica said.

He glanced over at her. "No?"

"With all due respect, Captain Wilder, that's not my business."

"Yet knowing I am a former SEAL was?"

"Any good officer worth their salt tries to find out who they're serving under. The reasons you left the SEALs or aren't active in missions any longer is not my concern. Some things are better left unsaid."

His cheeks flushed crimson and she wondered if she'd pushed it too far.

"You're right. Well, I may be retired from the SEALs, but I still oversee some of their training. Anything to keep involved."

Erica nodded. "A fine thing to be involved with."

Thorne smiled again, just briefly. "Well, I don't want to keep you from your run. If you continue on down the beach, there's another nice path which wraps around the hospital and forks, one path leading into the village and the other back to base. If you have the time, be sure to check out the village and in particular the temple."

"Thank you, Captain."

"When we're off duty, you can call me Thorne."

Now it was Erica's turn to blush. It came out of the blue; it caught her off guard.

Maybe it was supposed to.

"I'm not sure I'm comfortable with that."

"What harm is there in it?"

She didn't see any harm. When she went on shore leave with other shipmates or was off duty she didn't address them so formally. What was the difference here? The difference was she was never attracted to any of them, had never seen them so vulnerable and exposed.

"I'll think about it."

He cocked an eyebrow. "I have to say, I'm hurt. Am I so monstrous?"

"No." Erica grinned. "I only address my friends so informally."

"I'm not your friend?"

Now it was her turn to cock an eyebrow. "Really? You're asking me if we're friends?"

"I guess I am." He took a step closer to her and her pulse raced. She'd thought he was handsome when she'd first seen him, but that was when he'd been injured. Now he was healthy, towering over her and so close. She was highly attracted to him, she couldn't deny that. He stirred something deep inside her, something she hadn't felt in a long time.

Yearning.

There had been a couple other men since Captain Seaton, but not many, and none in the Navy. She didn't have time or interest.

Until she met Thorne.

Thorne was dangerous and, being her commanding officer, he was very taboo.

"We barely know each other, Captain. How can we be friends?"

"Easy. We can start by using our given names. I'm Thorne." And then he took her hand in his. It was strong and sent a shock of electricity through her.

Get a grip on yourself.

She needed to rein this in. This was how she'd fallen for Captain Seaton. He'd wooed her. She'd been blinded by hero worship, admiration, and she wouldn't let that happen again.

"We're not friends," Erica said quickly.

"We can be." His blue eyes twinkled mischievously. He was playing with her and she didn't like it. Thorne ran so hot and cold. He was trying to manipulate her.

"I don't think so, Captain." She suppressed a chuckle of derision and jogged past him, laughing to herself as she continued her run down the beach and perfectly aware that his eyes were on her.

Thorne watched her jog away and he couldn't help but admire her. Not many had stood up to him. He had the reputation of being somewhat of a jerk, to put it politely. He'd always been tough as nails. As Liam had always said. Yet Liam had gone straight into Special Ops and Thorne had become a medic. He wasn't without feelings.

He hadn't always been so closed off, but when you saw your identical twin brother lying broken on the ground after an insurgent attack, after he'd pushed you out of the way, then pieces of you died. Locking those parts of him away, the parts which still mourned his brother, was the only way to survive.

The only way to continue the fight, so that his brother's death wasn't in vain.

Thorne had hardened himself and, in doing so, had driven so many people away. They kept out of his way, they knew not to mess with him or challenge him. It was better that way. No one to care about. He didn't deserve it.

Erica was different.

You knew that when you approved her request to come to Okinawa.

His commanding officer still talked about the courage it had taken to stand up to him during that covert operation. How Erica had been adamant that Thorne was to remain on the USNV *Hope.* It had impressed Mick and that was hard to do.

Perhaps in Erica he'd met his match?

She's off-limits.

He needed that internal reminder that Erica was indeed off-limits. Thorne couldn't let another person in. There was no room for someone else in his life, so he had to get all these foolish notions out of his head.

Except, that was hard to do when he saw her, because those hazy, jangled memories from that time flooded his dreams—only now she wasn't just some ghost. The face was clear, tangible, and all he had to do was reach out and touch her to realize that his angel was indeed on Earth.

"Captain!" The shouts from the water caught his attention and he tore his gaze from Erica and out to sea.

The few men who had been doing their training were trying with futility to drag one of their comrades from the water, but the waves were making it difficult and the crimson streak following the injured man made Thorne's stomach knot.

Shark.

It was one of the dangers of training in the sea, though attacks were rare.

His first instinct was to run into the fray to help, but he

couldn't step foot into water. His prosthesis had robotic components and it would totally fry his leg. He needed his prosthetic leg to continue his job.

He was useless.

So useless.

He pulled out his phone and called for an ambulance, then ran after Erica, who wasn't far away.

"Erica!" he shouted, each step causing pain to shoot up his thigh. He hadn't run in so long. "Commander."

Erica stopped and turned, her eyes wide and eyebrows arched with curiosity. Without having to ask questions, she looked past him to the blood in the water and men struggling to bring their friend safely ashore.

She ran straight to them, whipping off her tank top to use as a tourniquet, wading into the surf without hesitation to aid the victim, while all he could do was stand there and watch in envy.

Only for a moment, though, before he shook off that emotion.

He might not be able to help in the same way as Erica, but he'd do everything he could. As soon as they had the man out of the water and on the beach, Thorne dropped down on one knee to survey the damage to the man's calf.

"What happened?" Thorne asked, not taking his eyes off the wound as Erica tightened the tourniquet made out of her Navy-issue tank top.

"We were swimming back in and Corporal Ryder fell behind. It was then he cried out. We managed to scare the shark off," one of Corporal Ryder's comrades responded.

"My leg!" Corporal Ryder screamed. "My leg is gone."

Thorne's throat constricted and his phantom leg twinged with agony, which almost caused him to collapse in pain.

You're fine. Your leg is gone. There is no pain.

"Your leg is there, Corporal," Erica responded. "You hear me? Your leg is there."

Corporal Ryder howled in agony and then cursed before going into shock.

"Lie him down, he's going into shock." Thorne reached out and helped Erica get Corporal Ryder down.

Erica was helping the other recruits assess Corporal Ryder's ABCs, the water still lapping against them as they worked on the leg, and Thorne stood there useless because he couldn't get his prosthetic leg wet; the corporal was still half in the water.

"How bad?" Thorne directed his question to Erica.

"We can probably salvage the leg. We won't know until we get him into surgery."

The ambulance from the hospital pulled up in the parking lot. Two paramedics were hurrying down the hill to the beach with a stretcher.

"Well, Commander Griffin, it looks like we're both scrubbing in. I don't know how many shark attacks you've seen…"

"Enough," she said, interrupting him, her expression soft. "Thank you for letting me assist you, Captain Wilder."

Thorne nodded and stood, getting out of the way as the paramedics arrived. "Commander, you go with the paramedics in the ambulance. I'll be there shortly."

There was no way he could keep up with the stretcher.

He'd get there in enough time.

Corporal Ryder needed all the help he could get.

Erica nodded and, as the ABCs of the corporal's condition were completed, he was on the gurney, headed toward the ambulance.

Thorne stayed behind with the other men, his stump throbbing, phantom pain racking him as his own body remembered the trauma he'd suffered.

He needed a moment to get it together.

To lock it all out, so he could be of some use to the corporal and help save that man's leg, where his own hadn't been.

CHAPTER FOUR

"MORE SUCTION."

Erica glanced up from the corporal's leg wound, but only briefly, as she carefully suctioned around the artery.

"Thank you, Commander," Thorne responded.

Their eyes locked across the surgical table. Even though she'd been here two weeks she had yet to operate with Thorne. When he had stitched his own leg, Erica had admired the work, given the condition and the crude tools he'd used. Now, watching him in action in a fully equipped and modern OR was something of beauty. She was so impressed with his surgical skill. There was a fluid grace with his hands, like a fine musician's, as he worked over the corporal's calf.

It was a simple wound to the leg, if you could call a shark bite simple. It didn't need or require two seasoned trauma surgeons, but Thorne had requested she be in there with him.

"You triaged him in the field. You have the right to be there too, Commander."

Even though she wasn't needed and it was her day off, Erica went into surgery with Captain Wilder against her better judgment. He'd been accommodating, but she still had a feeling that she was being scrutinized, manipulated, and that one wrong move and he'd send her packing. Well, maybe not personally send her packing, but she was sure he'd expedite it.

He probably wants to make sure you don't hack off Corporal Ryder's leg like you did to his.

Erica *tsked* under her breath, annoyed she'd let that thought in.

"Is something wrong, Commander?" Thorne asked.

"No, nothing. Why?"

"I thought you might have been annoyed about working on your day off. I know I've been pretty hard on you since you've arrived."

"No, I'm not complaining—far from it."

"You were huffing."

Erica glanced up again. Thorne's blue eyes twinkled slightly in what she could only assume was devilry.

What was that old saying her grandma had had? *Keep away from men who are* de pouille *or who are* possede. *They're just as bad as* rocachah.

Or, *keep away from men who are a mess or mischievous children. They're like beach burrs.* Erica had thought at the time her *mamère*'s advice was a bit nuts, but Captain Seaton certainly had been a *peekon* in her side and Thorne had the look of a *possede* for sure.

Great. I'm now channeling Mamère.

"I wasn't huffing over the work. The work, I love."

"Yet something rankled you."

"Why are you being so *tête dure*?" Then she gasped, realizing some of her Cajun had slipped out.

"So what?" Thorne asked, amused.

"*Tête dure* is stubborn, persistent and hardheaded. I'm from Louisiana."

"Really? I wouldn't have guessed it."

Erica rolled her eyes. "Don't judge a bed by its blanket."

"You mean a book by its cover?"

"Whatever."

"So why are you huffing?"

"Why are you being persistent?" she asked.

"Why not? I am the commanding officer of Trauma. I want to make sure those under my command..." He trailed off and Erica's stomach twisted. Was he alluding to her past in Rhode Island again?

Not everyone is out to get you. Just because one commanding officer accused you based on what happened to Dad doesn't mean they all will. Captain Dayton hadn't.

Then why did he keeping hinting at it? Maybe it was some kind of psychological warfare. Not that Thorne was at war with her. Perhaps it was some kind of SEAL training? It probably was and she shouldn't take it personally.

Erica cleared her throat. "If you want to know the reason I'm *tsking*, which is totally different from huffing, the reason is the wound. He's pretty mangled."

Thorne sighed. "His dreams of being in the Special Ops are over."

"He's lucky it didn't sever his femoral artery or we would have lost him on the beach." Erica continued to work, her hands moving as fast as Thorne's, working to repair the damage. It was an automatic process, one she didn't have to think too hard about. "More people die being trampled by hippos than by shark attacks."

"Hippos, Commander?" There were a few bewildered looks in the OR.

"Twenty-nine-hundred people annually."

"You're joking. That can't be right."

"It is. Look it up."

"Hippos?"

Erica chuckled. "I know, right?"

"Do you think the leg is salvageable?" Thorne asked, changing the subject.

"Yes." Their gaze locked again for a brief instant. The intensity of that shared moment made her think he wanted to ask her why his, which hadn't been as mangled, hadn't been saved.

She'd wanted to save his leg, but the infection had been too virulent.

Still, she'd always thought about him. What had happened to him, that gorgeous, brave Navy SEAL who had begged her. Who had called her beautiful.

"Like an angel."

Erica tried not to let those memories back in, but it was a failure. Hot flames of blood rushed up into her cheeks and she was thankful for the surgical mask. She broke the connection, her pulse racing.

You can't have this. He'll turn on you like Seaton did.

"I think Corporal Ryder, barring any post-op infection, will keep his leg," she said.

"Infection. Yes." His words were icy. "Well, look at this."

Erica glanced up and in his forceps there was a milky-colored sharp object, which looked like a bone fragment.

"What is that? Did it come off his femur?"

"It's a shark's tooth." The corners of his eyes crinkled with a smile obscured by his mask. He placed the tooth in the basin. "That will be something the corporal will want to keep."

"Like a badge of honor," Erica chuckled.

Thorne laughed quietly. "That, or he'll be out hunting the shark that ended his career prematurely."

"You don't think so?"

Thorne nodded. "Corporal Ryder has it in him. He had a passion to be in Special Ops; he's going to be annoyed."

"His life was saved. The animal didn't do it on purpose."

"It doesn't matter," Thorne snapped. "You don't know what it's like to be in such an elite force, protecting your country. Nothing else matters. You endure endless hours of torment to train, to make your body ready for the most treacherous conditions, and you gladly do it. You'd gladly lay down your life for a chance to keep your country free."

"Very patriotic," Erica said, trying to control her annoyance. "I may not be part of that elite crew, but what I do serves my country as well. I feel the same way."

"It's not the same. He'll have a bone to pick with that shark. You mark my words."

"So, would you?"

"Would I what?" Thorne asked, not looking at her.

"Go after the person or animal that ruined your career."

Thorne cleared his throat. "I did."

There was something in his tone which made her shudder, like she was in danger, but probably not in the same kind of danger as the shark.

This was something different. This kind of danger made her heart beat a bit faster, made her skin hot and made her feel like she was already the cornered prey animal with its throat exposed, waiting for the predator to make its kill. She didn't think Thorne wanted to kill her, far from it—but what he wanted from her, she didn't know.

Get revenge on her? Bring her to her knees?

She had no idea.

It was the kind of danger which excited her and terrified her.

It was the kind of danger she didn't run from. It was the kind she stood up to and she was ready for whatever was to come.

Thorne watched Erica as she checked on Corporal Ryder's vitals. Ryder had developed a post-op fever and had been in the ICU since he'd come out of surgery. He hadn't even fully come out of the anesthetic.

"My leg. My leg. Oh, God. Please, no!"

That was what Ryder had been screaming as they'd

pulled him from the water. He'd been screaming at the top of his lungs. Even though they'd all assured Ryder that his leg was still there, that it was attached and could be saved, it was like the young man had made up his mind that it wasn't going to happen.

Thorne had seen that before—when the spirit just wanted to give up and no amount of modern medicine would help that patient recover. It was like the soul was already trying to escape.

"Hold on, Liam. Just hold on."

"I can't, Thorne. Let me go."

"Why did you step in front of the IED for me?"

Thorne had read his own records, the ones which had been taken by his commanding officer from the USNV. He'd developed a post-op fever, no doubt from the virulent infection coursing through his body.

In his brief memories, when he could recall that moment, he remembered the feeling of slipping away, but something pulling him back.

An angel.

Erica.

Seeing her face hovering above him had grounded him.

Sometimes when the pain was bad, when it felt like the amputated leg was still there and he couldn't take it any longer, he hated Erica for saving his life.

Then again, after he'd been shot and they'd spent those days holed up in the sewers, he hadn't thought he was going to get out of there. He'd thought he was going to die in the sewer, which would've been better.

One less body in a casket for his mother to weep over.

No, don't let those memories in.

He didn't want to think about his twin's funeral, because when he thought of Liam he inevitably thought about how he'd tried to save his life.

"You're crushing me, Thorne."

"I'm applying pressure. I'm the medic, you're the hero. Remember?"

Liam had smiled weakly. *"I'm past that point. Let me go."*

That moment of clarity, when you felt no pain and your body was just tired of struggling on. You weren't afraid of death any longer. Death meant rest.

Thorne glanced back at the ICU. He saw that look of resolution on Corporal Ryder's face and he hoped the young man would fight.

Ryder still had his leg.

Thorne didn't and if he hadn't been in the medical corps of the Navy, if he hadn't had so many commendations and something to fall back on, he would've been discharged.

Ryder has to live.

Thorne clenched his fists to ease the anger he was feeling, because if he marched in there now to do his own assessment of the situation, to ease the guilt and anguish he was feeling over Corporal Ryder, he was likely to take it out on Erica.

The surgeon who had taken his leg. Only, she'd tried to save it. He'd seen the reports. It was the infection from the dirty water he'd been forced to live in.

There was nothing to be done at that point. There had been no one to blame but himself. He was the one who'd decided to step in front of that bullet to protect Tyler.

He didn't blame Erica—only, maybe, for saving his life.

He'd thought about her countless times, about kissing those lips, touching her face. Of course, those had been fantasies as he'd recovered. He thought those feelings of lust would disappear when he met her in person.

Thorne was positive that he'd built her up in his head. That it was the drugs which had obscured his memories.

No one could be that beautiful.

He was wrong. Even though his memory had been slightly fuzzy, his fantasies about her didn't do her justice.

When she'd rushed into the fray to give Corporal Ryder first aid on the beach, he knew why she was one of the top trauma surgeons in the medical corps.

The real woman was so much more than his fantasy one. Which was dangerous, because he felt something more than just attraction...

It was dangerous, because he did feel something more than just attraction toward her. He wanted to get to know her, open his heart to her, and that was something he couldn't do.

He wasn't going to let in any one else.

There was no room to love. He wouldn't risk his heart, and if something happened to him, well, he wasn't going to put any woman through that. He'd seen what had happened to his brother's wife and children when Liam had died. And, make no mistake, it was his fault Liam had died.

Thorne couldn't do that to anyone else.

So these emotions Erica was stirring in him scared him.

He'd been alone almost a decade and managed. What he needed to do was get control of himself. Then he could work with her.

No problem.

Yeah. Right.

He headed into the ICU, sliding the isolation door shut behind him. Erica glanced up at him briefly as she continued to write in Ryder's chart.

"Captain," she said offhandedly, greeting him.

"Commander," Thorne acknowledged, moving to the far side of the bed to put a distance between them. "How's he doing?"

"Stable." She said the word in a way that made Thorne think being stable was sufficient and in some cases—especially this one, where it wasn't even as serious as other wounds—stable should've been enough.

"Any sign of infection?"

"No." Her cheeks flushed briefly.

"Well, that's good. If the wound becomes infected and he doesn't respond to antibiotics we'll have to amputate."

She looked at him. "You have an obsession with amputation."

"Can you blame me?" And even though he knew he shouldn't, and even though he knew she already knew his leg was gone, he bent over and rolled up his scrub leg. "Titanium."

Their gazes locked and his pulse was pounding in his ears. He waited to see if she would admit to it. On one hand, he hoped she would and on the other hand, he hoped she wouldn't, but how long could they keep up this facade?

"I know," she said quietly without batting an eyelash, before she turned to her chart.

Thorne was stunned she admitted to it. When they'd first met again here in Okinawa she'd acted like she didn't remember him, just as he'd pretended he didn't recall her.

He smoothed down the scrubs over his prosthetic leg and then straightened up. The tension in the room was palpable. Usually, tension never bothered him and he thrived in high-stress situations, but this was different.

Against his better judgment, and under the guise that he wanted to see Corporal Ryder's charts, he moved behind her. Which was a mistake. Her hair smelled faintly like coconuts. He was so close he could reach out and touch her, run his fingers through her short honey-colored hair. He resisted and instead took the chart from her, flipping through it.

"Just a fever, then?"

"Y-yes," she stuttered. "Yes, a fever. There shouldn't be

a reason why his vitals are just stable, because they were just that. One small change…"

Thorne stepped away from her. "I understand. As long as there isn't infection."

He didn't look at her, but he got the sense she wanted to say more, and he wanted her to say more.

"You know," she whispered, her voice shaking a bit with frustration.

Good. He wanted her to hate him. It would be easier. *Hate me.*

"Yes." He handed her back the chart. Thorne knew she was annoyed. It was good that she was, maybe then she'd avoid him. If she hated him, then he'd be less tempted to want her. There would be little chance of them ever being together, which was for the best.

Yeah. Tell yourself another lie, why don't you?

"Looks good, Commander Griffin. Keep me updated on any changes in the corporal's status." He turned and left the ICU, trying to put a safe distance between the two of them.

The hiss of the isolation room's door behind him let him know she was following him. Why did he think she wouldn't follow him? From the little he knew of Commander Erica Griffin, he knew she wasn't the kind of officer to take anything lying down.

He was in for a fight.

She grabbed his arm to stop him. "I don't think we're done talking, Captain Wilder."

They were standing right in front of the busy nurses' station, where a few nurses stopped what they were doing. Even though they weren't looking their way, he could tell they were listening in earnest.

Not many officers stood up to him.

"Commander, I don't think this is the time or the place to bring it up."

"Oh, it's the time and place." She glared at some of the nurses and then grabbed him by his arm and dragged him into an on-call room, shutting the door behind her, locking it.

"Commander, what's the meaning of this?" he asked, trying to keep his voice firm. He didn't like the idea of being locked in a dark on-call room with her.

Especially when his blood was still thrumming with wanting her.

"I think you know exactly the meaning of this. Why did you pretend you didn't remember me?"

"You did the same."

Her eyes narrowed. "Only because I thought you didn't remember me for the last two weeks."

He cocked an eyebrow. "So that justifies lying to me?"

She snorted. "I never lied to you. However, you lied to me."

"Why didn't you say anything to me?" He took a step toward her, though he knew very well he should keep his distance.

"Why would I? If you weren't going to mention the traumatic experience, I wasn't about to bring it up again."

"Perhaps you felt guilty." He was baiting her, pushing her buttons.

Hate me. Loathe me.

She advanced toward him. "I don't feel guilty for saving your life. I did what had to be done. You would've died if I hadn't taken your leg. You're a doctor, and I'm sure you've had access to the chart which magically disappeared off the ship when you were taken, so you know I had no choice—I don't regret what I did. Given the choice again, if it meant saving a life and having someone hate me for the choice I made, I would cut off your leg to save your life."

Thorne took a step back, impressed with her, but also

annoyed that he was even more drawn to her and her strength.

He didn't know how to reply to that.

Didn't know what to say.

Suddenly there was someone pounding on the door.

"Commander Griffin, it's Corporal Ryder... He's crashing."

Suddenly there was nothing left to say. Erica flung open the door and both of them sped toward the ICU, the sound of a flatline becoming deafening, and everything else was forgotten.

CHAPTER FIVE

Erica flipped the tooth over, like it was a poker chip, staring at it morosely as she sat at a bar, which reminded her of *Gilligan's Island*, complete with bamboo huts, tikis and coconut shells. It was like a throwback to something from the sixties.

Normally, she wouldn't occupy a bar or pub, but tonight she needed company.

She needed a drink and this was the closest place to her quarters.

Besides, she'd never had a whiskey and cola adorned with a pink umbrella and glittery streamers before. Her drink reminded her of her first bike, which had had the same streamers. At least her drink didn't have spokey-dokes. The Bar Painappurufeisu, which she believed translated to "Pineapple Face," served alcohol and that was all that mattered at the moment.

"Scooby, hit me again," she called to the barkeep.

Scooby nodded and smiled, probably not really understanding what she was saying, and said, "No problem," before heading down to the other end of the bar.

Erica giggled again.

She definitely needed to lay off the liquor. She rarely indulged and this was what she got for that. She was a lightweight and laughing at everything.

At least if she was laughing she wasn't thinking about what had happened to Corporal Ryder. Then she glanced down at the shark's tooth in her palm and slammed it against the counter.

"To hell with it, Scooby. I need another drink."

"No problem," Scooby answered from the end of the bar.

"Don't you think you've had enough?"

Erica glanced over and saw that Thorne had sat down beside her.

Just what she needed. Someone else whose life she'd ruined. She wasn't a surgeon—she was apparently no better than the grim reaper.

"Scooby will let me know when I've had enough."

A smile twitched on Thorne's face. "The only English Scooby knows is what kind of drink you want, monetary value and 'no problem'."

Scooby looked up and gave a thumbs-up. "No problem."

Erica moaned and rubbed her forehead. "Great. I've been rattling off to him about various things."

Thorne shrugged. "He's a good listener. It's his job. Although, he was a fisherman before the base sprung up."

"I thought most Okinawans knew English."

"Most do. Scooby doesn't; he only learned what he needed to know."

Erica narrowed her eyes. She didn't believe a word Thorne was saying, though that could be the liquor talking.

"You don't believe me?" he asked, his eyes twinkling.

"Why should I? Since I arrived you've questioned me, *lied* to me and generally have been a pain in my butt. No offense, Captain."

"None taken, Commander."

Erica turned back to her drink, playing with the many

glittery decorations. Her body tensed, being so close to Thorne. It wasn't because he was her commanding officer; that didn't bother her in the least. It wasn't because she'd taken his leg; she knew she'd made the right medical decision. It was because she was drawn to him and she shouldn't be. Captain Wilder was off-limits and it annoyed her that she was allowing herself to feel this way. That he affected her so.

Especially today.

"What do you have there?" Thorne asked, though she had a feeling he already knew.

She set it down on the countertop anyway: the shark tooth, gleaming and polished under the tiki lighting.

"Why do you have that?" he asked.

"I didn't think it should go to medical waste. I know we were saving it for..." She couldn't even finish her sentence. She was a doctor, a surgeon and she was used to death. People did die, and had died on her, but usually only when they were too far gone.

Thorne had been worse, yet he was here, beside her. Alive.

Corporal Ryder's death shook her because his death shouldn't have happened. It boggled her mind. She cupped the shark tooth in her palm again, feeling its jagged edge against her skin.

Thorne reached over, opened her fingers, exposing her palm, and took the shark tooth from her.

His touch made her blood ignite. A spark of electricity zipped through her veins.

Pull your hand away.

Only, she liked the touch. She needed it at this moment.

"Let me see that," he said gently. Erica watched him, watched his expression as he looked over the tooth carefully. "Can I keep it?"

"Why?" she asked.

"I knew him—he has a younger brother. Perhaps I'll send it to him if he wants it."

"Sure." She picked at the paper napkin under her drink. It was soaked with condensation and came apart easily. "Did you get a hold of Corporal Ryder's family?"

Thorne nodded slowly. "I did."

"I don't have any siblings." Erica wasn't sure why she was telling him that.

"That's too bad."

She nodded at the tooth again. "Do you think that's something his family would want? I mean...under the circumstances."

"I think so. Though, the flag at his state burial will mean more."

Erica sighed sadly. "There was no reason for him to die."

"He was attacked by a shark."

"It was a simple wound. It didn't even sever the artery."

"You know as well as I do that sometimes there are things beyond our control as physicians. If he gave up the will to live... I've seen it so many times. Even if you fight so hard to save a life, if that person has decided that they're going to die there's nothing you can do."

Erica nodded.

It was true. She knew it. She'd seen it herself so many times, but Ryder's death was so senseless. He would've made a full recovery. Sure, he wouldn't have been able to continue his training to become an elite member of the SEALs, but he also wouldn't have been discharged from the Navy.

Was that worth dying over? Was that what had driven Ryder just to give up?

Was that why Dad just gave up? How much pain had he been in?

She sighed, thinking about him. Her father had had a

loving family; he'd often told Erica she was the light in his life. Yet it hadn't been enough.

She hadn't been enough.

"Did they say what caused his death?" she asked, hoping Thorne could give her a more tangible answer.

"No, but there will be a postmortem, and maybe then we can get an answer. I'm thinking that the drugs, the shock of the attack and surgery was just too much of a strain on him. It's rare, but it does happen."

Erica nodded. "Well, why don't you join me and drink to Corporal Ryder's memory."

"Is that what you're doing?" he asked.

She nodded. "Oh, yeah."

"Then I'd love to join you, but you made it clear we can't be friends."

Erica winced. "I overreacted. I'm sorry. We can be friends."

"Okay." He motioned to Scooby who brought him a stubby-looking bottle.

"What's that?" she asked, because she couldn't read the Japanese on the label.

"It's beer. I don't know what kind, but it's damn good."

"I didn't know the Japanese brewed beer."

"You should've done your research before you took a posting in Okinawa prefect, then."

Erica snorted. "I did my research, I just somehow missed that."

"Okay, what do you know?"

She looked at him strangely. "Are you testing me?"

Thorne shrugged. "Why not? You said you studied."

Erica shook her head and pinched the bridge of her nose. "What part of 'pain in my butt' didn't you get?"

"Haven't you ever heard of a pub quiz before?"

"Really?"

Thorne chuckled. "Okay, fine. Although the prize would've been totally worth it."

"Prize?" Erica asked. "Now I'm intrigued. What would be my prize?"

He grinned. "Play and find out."

Just walk away.

The prize was probably something not worth it. Or something totally inappropriate—not that she would mind being inappropriate with Thorne, if he hadn't been her commanding officer; if they didn't have a history as surgeon and patient. Yet here she was, falling into this sweet trap again.

He's not Seaton. They're not all Seaton.

Which was true, but after a couple of drinks she was willing to let her guard down. *It's the booze.*

And maybe it was completely innocuous. Perhaps he was just being kind and just trying to get her mind off the fact that they'd lost someone today. Someone who shouldn't have died.

Since when has Captain Wilder ever been nice to you?

That was the truth. He hadn't been overly friendly or warm since she'd arrived at the base. Even when he'd been her patient he'd called her names and told her not to take his leg.

He didn't have the sunniest disposition.

"Like an angel."

That blasted moment again, sneaking into her mind, making her thoughts all jumbled and confused. She should just walk away, but she was too intrigued not to find out what the prize was. Besides, when was the last time she'd backed away from a challenge? If it was something inappropriate she could tell him where to go; they were off duty.

Still, she wasn't here because of a lark.

"I don't think it's appropriate."

"Because of Corporal Ryder?" Thorne asked.

"Yeah. Maybe I should just call it a night." She got up to leave, but he reached out and grabbed her arm, stopping her from leaving.

"Don't go," he said.

Erica sat down. "Okay, but I have to say I'm not in much of a jovial mood. Prize or not."

Thorne chuckled. "Tell you what, you'll still get your prize."

"And what would that be?"

"A tour around Ginowan and the countryside. You could test your knowledge."

Erica couldn't help but smile. When Thorne wanted to be, he was charming. "I don't think that's wise."

"Why?"

She didn't know how to answer that truthfully.

Because I don't want to be alone with you. Because my career is more important.

Because I'm weak.

"I don't think that's wise. You're my commanding officer."

Thorne's face remained expressionless. "You're right. Of course you're right."

Even though he didn't show any sign of anger, there was tension in his voice and possibly a sense of rejection. She knew that tone well enough from other guys she'd turned down, because there just wasn't time for romance.

And because you're frightened.

Erica stood. "I should go. Good night, Captain Wilder."

Thorne nodded but didn't look at her. "I'll see you in the morning, Commander Griffin."

Thorne watched her leave the bar; even though he shouldn't, he did. It was good that she'd turned him down. He didn't know what had come over him.

Probably the beer.

"You're looking for trouble with that one," Scooby said.

Thorne snorted. "I'm not looking for trouble."

"Good, because that one is strong willed. Why did you tell her I can't speak English?"

Thorne chuckled. "I was playing with her."

"Ay-ay-ay. Perhaps I should warn her off of you, Captain Wilder. Perhaps you're nothing but trouble." Scooby smiled and set another bottle of beer down on the counter. "I'm sorry to hear about the corporal. He was a good man."

"He was."

"I would like to send something to his family." Scooby reached behind the bar and pulled out a picture. "This was from last month. Corporal Ryder led our bowling team to victory."

Thorne smiled at the picture of Scooby, Corporal Ryder and some other officers in horrific bright-orange bowling shirts holding up matching color marble balls.

"I'm sure they'd like that."

Scooby nodded and walked away. Thorne carefully placed the framed picture down and then set the shark tooth on top of it.

Damn you, Ryder.

"You hold on, Liam. Do you hear me?"

"I hear you."

"It's not as bad as you think. You can live."

Liam shook his head. "No, little brother."

"Stop calling me little. I'm three minutes younger than you."

Liam chuckled, his pupils dilating, his breathing shallow. "You'll always be my little brother, Thorne. Remember that."

Thorne cursed under his breath and finished off his beer. He didn't want to think about Liam right now.

When do you ever?

It was true. Since Liam had died in his arms, he didn't like to think about him.

But then, who would want to think about a loved one they couldn't save?

One who could've been saved.

One that would still have been alive if he hadn't made such a foolish mistake.

CHAPTER SIX

Damn and double damn.

Erica turned on her heel and tried to walk away as fast as she could, even though the little voice inside her head told her that she couldn't avoid Captain Wilder for the rest of her life. She was his second in command.

Needless to say, she was damn well going to try.

"Commander Griffin—a word, if you will."

Erica grimaced and cursed under her breath.

Damn.

She turned around slowly as Thorne walked toward her. He wasn't wearing his usual scrubs; he was in uniform. Not the full dress and not the fatigues—the service khaki and it didn't look half bad on him.

The khaki brought out the brilliant blue color in his eyes.

Damn.

"Of course, Captain Wilder. How can I help you?"

He shook his head. "Not here. Let's go to my office."

Erica's stomach knotted. Oh, great. What was going to happen to her now? Last time she'd been involved with a commanding officer she'd been sent packing. That was why she didn't mix work and relationships.

They walked in silence to his office. He opened the door for her.

"Please have a seat."

"I prefer to stand, if you don't mind, Captain."

Thorne frowned. "Why are you standing at attention, Commander?"

"Aren't I being called up on the rug?"

"It's called 'out on the carpet'. I think that's what you mean."

Erica sighed. "Right."

"No, Commander. You're not being scolded. At ease."

She relaxed, but not completely. This time she wasn't going to be caught unawares. This time she'd be ready for whatever Captain Wilder had for her. Erica planned to keep this commission. She wasn't going to be run out of another one. Not this time. Since her Rhode Island posting, when her reputation had been left in tatters, she'd worked damned hard to get it back. It was her prize intangible possession. Her reputation was at stake and that was all she had left.

"You can sit, Commander."

"I still prefer to stand, Captain."

"I'd prefer it if you'd sit."

"Why?" she asked.

"I never sit in the presence of a lady who remains standing. It's how I was raised. So if you would sit, then I could sit—and I'd really like to sit because my leg has been bothering me something fierce today."

Erica could see the discomfort etched in his face, the barely controlled pain. His knuckles were white as he was gripping the back of his chair and there was a fine sheen of sweat across his brow. It wasn't about nicety; he was suffering.

"I'm sorry, Captain."

He shook his head. "Don't be sorry, please just have a seat."

She nodded and sat down on the other side of his desk.

Even though he told her she wasn't being reprimanded, she was still ill at ease. She had no idea why Thorne wanted to see her.

Performance review?

One could only hope. She'd been at the job for a month now.

"Commander, I called you up here because I want to apologize."

What? "I'm sorry...what, Captain?"

"Apologize, Commander. It's not an easy thing for me to say, but that's why I called you up here."

"I'm not sure I quite understand."

"For making you feel uncomfortable at the bar two weeks ago and on the beach. I know the corporal's death affected you and it looked like you needed a friend. I'm sorry if my actions were out of line."

"Thank you, Captain." Erica was stunned. She'd never had a superior apologize to her before. It surprised her. There were many things she'd been expecting him to say, but an apology had not been one of them. "I'm sorry too."

Thorne cocked an eyebrow. "For what?"

"For avoiding you."

A smile broke out on his face, his eyes twinkling. "I knew you were."

"You did."

"You're not that aloof, Erica. May I call you Erica now?"

She nodded. "Yes. I think we've established that when we're alone that's acceptable."

"So, why have you been avoiding me?"

"I thought it was for the best. I'm here to prove myself. I'm not here to make friends."

"Everyone needs a friend."

"Not me." And she meant it.

"Really? I'm intrigued—you have no friends?"

Erica rolled her eyes. "I have friends, just not here. At home and not in the service." Well, except for Regina, but he didn't need to know that.

"I'm talking about friends here. You need a friend."

"And what about you?"

Thorne leaned back in his chair, tenting his fingers. "What about me?"

"Who are your friends, if you don't mind me asking? You work just as much as I do, if not more. I've been to Scooby's bar a couple of times and two weeks ago was the first time I saw you there."

"Scooby knows English, by the way."

"What?" she asked.

"I was pulling your leg, but he warned me that I should tell you the truth."

She rolled her eyes. "I don't know why I fell for that. I knew he knew English. He's been living around the base his whole life."

Thorne shrugged. "It's a bit of an initiation."

"I thought my crazy shifts at the beginning were that."

"Partly." He grinned. "It's true, I don't have many friends here, being the commanding officer of the trauma department and being involved in Special Ops training. Well, as much as I can be with my prosthetic. I can't do much in the way of water training."

"We can be friends." Erica was stunned when the words slipped out of her mouth and she could tell Thorne was just as surprised.

"Really? After that whole rigmarole you just gave me about being here to prove yourself and not make friends?"

She smiled. "Perhaps you're wearing me down. Perhaps I do need a friend."

Their gazes locked and she could feel the blood rushing to her cheeks; hear her pulse thunder in her ears.

You're weak. So weak.

"I'm glad," he said, finally breaking the tension which crackled between them. "Very glad. So I can assume my apology is accepted."

"Yes."

"Good. So were you really avoiding me because you didn't want to be friends or was it something else? You know, I used to interrogate people in the Special Ops. I know when someone is lying to me." He got up and moved toward her, sitting on the edge of his desk in front of her. Their bodies were so close, but not quite touching.

Get a grip on yourself.

"Fine. I was avoiding you because I thought perhaps you might've been coming on to me."

"And if I was?"

Flames licked through her body.

"Then it would be inappropriate," she said, meeting his gaze. "It would be unwelcome."

No. It wouldn't.

Thorne nodded and moved away. "Good, because I wasn't—and I wanted to make sure you weren't avoiding me because you thought I was being inappropriate with you, Commander."

She should be glad, but she wasn't. If Thorne wasn't her captain or her former patient…if she hadn't seen him at his most vulnerable… Well, there was no point in dwelling on the past. The past couldn't be changed and there was no possible hope or future with Thorne. None. He was off-limits.

"I'm glad to hear that." She stood. "May I get back to my duties? I was about to start rounds."

"Of course. But, look, my offer still stands about taking you around Ginowan. As friends. I think it would do you good to get off the base and see some sights. I know you're used to working on a ship where there weren't many escape options."

"Thank you. I would like that."

He nodded. "It'll do you good to get out there. We'll meet tomorrow at zero nine hundred hours. You're dismissed, Commander."

Erica saluted and left his office posthaste. Not because she was late for rounds, but because once again she found she had to put some distance between her and Thorne. Why did he have to be her commanding officer? Why was she even thinking about him in that way? She'd lost her prestigious posting in Rhode Island because she'd dated a commanding officer and when it had gone south she'd been thrown under the bus.

"Lieutenant Griffin is mentally unfit to become a commander. Look what happened to her father."

Men couldn't be trusted.

She didn't need this, yet he was right. Erica was lonely and, even though she tried to tell herself otherwise, she wanted the companionship Thorne was offering.

She wanted the friendship and maybe something more.

And that thought scared her.

Thorne pulled up in front of Erica's quarters in his tiny Japanese-made turbo. She had to suppress a giggle when she saw him because the car was so small and he was so tall.

He rolled down the window. "I'd open the door for you, but once I get behind the wheel it's a bit of a pain to get out and back in with my leg."

"No worries." She checked to make sure her door was locked and then headed for the car. She climbed into the passenger seat. She was five-ten and it was a squeeze for her too. So she could only imagine that Thorne might've needed a shoehorn to get his big Nordic frame into this little hatchback.

"I thought you would've driven an SUV or something," she said.

"Not in Okinawa. Some of the roads are narrow. I do have a nice, big gas-guzzling truck on my mom's farm back in Minnesota."

"Minnesota. That doesn't surprise me, given your Viking name."

He grinned. "Yes, my family is from Norway. Your name, though: it's hard to figure where you're from."

"I was a Navy brat, but my *mamère*—my grand-mother—lived in the bayous of Louisiana and I was born there."

"A Southern girl."

"Yes, sir. Though don't ask me to do a Creole accent or drawl or whatever. I don't have one. I was born in New Orleans, but I didn't live there very long. I was raised on the East and West Coasts. Except for a three-year stint in Arizona."

"Yet you blurt out some Cajun every once in a while."

"A bit. I spent a lot of summers with Mamère."

"You've been all over."

"Yes and working on a medical ship helped with that."

"I bet." He put the car into drive. "You haven't seen Okinawa yet."

"No. I haven't."

"You're in for a real treat, then."

He signaled and pulled away, down the road to the base's entrance. They signed out with the Master of Arms on duty. Once the gate lifted they were off down the road toward the city of Ginowan. The wind blew in her hair and she could smell the sea. She took a deep breath and relaxed. It was the first time in a long time she'd actually sat back and relaxed.

"Where are we headed?" she asked, not that she really

cared where they were going. She was just happy to be off the base and seeing the sights.

"There's a temple in Ginowan that's pretty. Thought we'd stop there first. Maybe we can spot some Shisa dogs."

"What are Shisa dogs?"

"They guard the island. There are stone carvings of lion dogs hidden everywhere."

"Neat."

Thorne nodded. "Not much of the original architecture remains. Most was destroyed in 1945 during the Battle of Okinawa in World War II."

"I did know that. My grandfather fought during that battle, actually."

"With the Navy?"

"No, the Marines."

"Did he survive?"

Erica chuckled. "Of course, or I wouldn't be here talking to you today. My father was the youngest of seven children and he wasn't born until 1956."

Thorne laughed. "Good point."

"Did any of your family serve?"

Thorne's easy demeanor vanished and he visibly tensed. His smile faded and that dour, serious face she was used to seeing around the halls of the base hospital glanced at her.

"Yes. My brother."

"Navy?"

"Yes." It was a clipped answer, like he didn't want to say anything further, and she wasn't going to press him, but she couldn't help but wonder where his brother was. Did he still serve? Was Thorne's brother in the SEALs? Maybe that was why it was a bit of a sore spot for him.

Either way, it wasn't her business.

Just like her past wasn't his business.

"So, tell me about these dogs."

Thorne's expression softened. "I'm no expert on Okinawan history. Your best bet is to ask Scooby."

"Oh, yes? The man who supposedly doesn't know English? 'That'll be no problem'," she air-quoted.

Thorne laughed with her. "Again, sorry about that."

"I know, I know. It was all a part of my initiation. I've had several now; I should be used to them."

"Scooby wants to warn you off of me and vice versa."

"Vice versa?" she asked. "Why? What have I ever done to him?"

"He thinks we're both too pigheaded and stubborn to get along well."

Erica chuckled. "He could be right. I am stubborn, but not without just cause."

"So I've heard."

Now she was intrigued and a bit worried. "From who?"

"My commanding officer. He said you were quite adamant that I not be removed from the ship, even if the orders came direct from the White House."

She laughed. "That's true. When it comes to my patients. Some find it annoying."

"Not me," Thorne said and he glanced over at her quickly. "It's the mark of a damn fine surgeon. Which you are."

Heat flamed in her cheeks. "Thank you."

"There's no need to thank me. I'm speaking the truth. I don't lie."

"That's funny," she said.

"What?"

"That you don't lie, when you *clearly* did." She regretted the words the moment she said them.

Good job. You are finally starting to make friends and you insult that one and only friend.

Instead of giving her the silent treatment he snorted. "I didn't really lie per se."

"How do you figure that?"

"I just withheld the truth."

Erica raised an eyebrow. "Right. And the definition of lying is…?"

Thorne just winked at her. "Here we are. I hope you wore socks. No shoes in the temple." He parked the car on the street and they climbed out. It was good to stretch her legs. The little temple was built into the side of a hill surrounded by an older part of town, which was bustling. The temple was overgrown with foliage and the stairs up to it were crumbling.

"It's beautiful." And it was. Erica had traveled around the world, and had seen many places of worship, but there was something about this temple which struck her as different and captivating. Something she couldn't quite put her finger on.

"Shall we go in?"

"Are we allowed to?" she asked.

"Sure." And then without asking her permission Thorne reached out and took her hand, sending a shock of electricity up her spine at his touch. He didn't seem to notice the way her breath caught in her throat when she gasped.

Instead he squeezed her hand gently and led her through the packed streets toward the temple. What was even weirder was that she didn't pull away.

She let him.

She liked the feeling of her hand in his. It was comforting, and in the few past relationships she'd had, she could never recall sharing such a moment of intimacy. There had been lust, sex, but hand-holding? Never. Such a simple act gave her a thrill.

Don't think like that. It means nothing. You're just friends.

Right. She had to keep reminding herself of that.

They were just friends.

That was all there was between them and that was all there could ever be.

CHAPTER SEVEN

THORNE DIDN'T KNOW why he reached out and took her hand to lead her across the busy Ginowan street. It was instinctive and a gentlemanly thing to do. They were halfway across the street when he realized that he was holding Erica's hand, that he was guiding her through the maze of people, whizzing motorbikes and cars toward the temple.

She didn't pull away either like she had before.

Erica let him lead her to safety. It was an act of trust and Thorne had a feeling that trust didn't come too easily to her.

Not that he blamed her. People couldn't always be trusted. He'd learned that well enough both in his service as a SEAL and a surgeon.

"Yes, Dr. Wilder. I quit smoking."

"No. I know nothing about threats to your country."

Thorne could usually read people like a book. It had been one of his strong suits when he was in the Special Ops. Erica was hard to read though and maybe that was another reason why he was *so* drawn to her.

He did like a challenge.

You shouldn't be thinking this way. She's your second in command. She made her feelings quite clear to you the other day.

She was a puzzle. One he wanted to figure out. He was

a sucker for puzzles. Thorne cursed himself. He couldn't be involved with her or any other woman.

He couldn't emotionally commit to someone.

Not in his line of work.

Not after seeing what it had done to his brother's widow, to his mother.

When he'd lost his leg and woken up in that hospital in San Diego, unaware of where he was and how he'd got there, his first memory besides Erica's face haunting him had been seeing his mom curled up on an uncomfortable cot, a few more gray strands in her black hair, dark circles under her eyes.

It had almost killed his mother when Liam had died.

No. He couldn't do that to someone else and he couldn't ever have kids either. He didn't want to leave his children without a father should something happen to him.

You're not in Special Ops anymore. What harm could happen here?

A shudder ran down his spine. What harm indeed? Corporal Ryder probably hadn't thought his life would end during a simple training exercise. That it would end because of a shark bite.

Take the risk.

It was a different voice in his head this time, one that he thought he'd long buried, and it wasn't welcome here now.

No. She's off-limits.

"I think it's going to rain," Erica said, glancing up at the sky.

"What?" Thorne asked. "Sorry, I didn't hear you."

"Rain. It became overcast quite quickly."

Thorne didn't look at the sky; he glanced at the delicate but strong hand in his. It felt good there, but it didn't belong. He let it go and jammed his hands into his pockets.

Her cheeks bloomed with pink and she awkwardly rubbed her hand, as if wiping away the memory of his.

"Maybe we should go inside," Thorne offered, breaking the tension between them.

"Sure," she agreed, but she wouldn't look at him. "Lead the way."

He nodded and led her up the walkway toward the temple entrance. This had to stop. She was affecting him so much. Usually he was so focused on his work. Now he was distracted and he knew he had to get control of this situation before it escalated any further. She'd agreed to be friends. They could be friends.

Who are you kidding?

He watched her as she made her way to the small, almost abandoned Ryukyuan temple. It was made of wood and stone and embedded in the side of a hill. It was more a tourist attraction than it was a functional temple, as most Okinawans practiced at home in honoring their ancestors.

She paused and touched the stone at the gate, glancing up, and her mouth slightly opened as she marveled at the architecture. It was old, mixed with new, as parts of the small temple had been destroyed during the battle of Okinawa.

"Beautiful." She smiled at him, her eyes twinkling and her honey-blond hair blowing softly in the breeze. She was weaving some sort of spell around him. He just wanted to take her in his arms and kiss her. The thought startled him because, even though it wasn't new, he'd been trying to ignore the desire, the lust which coursed through him. He didn't recall ever having this urgency before with women he dated in the past.

This need.

This want.

"I thought you wanted to get out of the rain?" Thorne asked.

"Right." She blushed and stopped at the door to take off her shoes and Thorne followed her, glad he was wearing slip-ons so he wouldn't have to struggle with laces and his leg.

"Welcome. You're welcome to look around; we just ask that there be no photography," the guide said from behind the desk as they entered the temple.

"Thank you." Thorne paid a donation to allow them in and explore the history of the temple. Erica was wandering around and looking at the carvings and the paintings on the wall.

"Are these the lion dogs you were talking about, Thorne?"

"Ah, yes," the guide said, standing. "The Shisa is a protective ward to keep out evil spirits. They're often found in pairs."

Thorne nodded and then moved behind Erica, placing his hand on the small of her back to escort her further into the temple, where a few other tourists were milling about, reading about the history and photographs on the walls.

Erica leaned over and whispered, her breath fanning his neck. "I really know nothing about Okinawa history."

"I know a bit."

"What religion do Okinawans practice?"

"There are several forms, but it all falls under the Ryukyuan religion. A lot of the worship has to do with nature."

Erica smiled. "Pretty awesome."

"I have some books for you to read, if you're interested."

"I don't have time to read." Then she moved away from him to look at some old pictures after the battle of Okinawa. "Crazy. They say it was the bloodiest battle of the Pacific War."

"It was and 149,193 of those lost were Okinawan civilians."

"Such a loss of life."

"It is," he said. "It's a hard line we walk as surgeons who serve. We don't like to see death, but yet we serve something bigger and greater. Something that helps innocents remain free."

Gooseflesh broke out over her at his eloquent words. She often felt at war with herself and her beliefs. Even though she was in the Navy she wasn't one who went out to fight. Though she'd learned about armed combat as part of her training during Annapolis, she hoped she'd never have to be in a situation to use it.

Thorne was different.

He'd actually served in combat situations.

He carried a gun and as a SEAL had undertaken covert operations that she couldn't even begin to imagine. She wanted to ask him if he'd ever killed someone before, but she could tell by the pain in his eyes when he read the names on the list, the names of those who had fallen during the Battle of Okinawa, that he had.

And it pained him.

Besides it wasn't her business to ask him that and she was enjoying his company; the last thing she wanted to do was drive him away by prying.

The moment he'd mentioned his brother he'd put a wall up.

"It is a hard line to walk," she said. She moved away from him into a hallway, which was carved. They were heading under the hillside and she could hear water running. When they got down at the end of the hallway there was a hole in the ceiling letting the light filter through and in the center was a pond where pots of incense were burning.

Misty rain fell through the opening, causing smoke to rise from the incense. It was beautiful, and the smell was spicy but welcoming.

"What's this?" Erica asked as she moved closer.

"It's called a Kaa, I believe. Water is holy, hence the incense."

"It's beautiful."

Thorne nodded. "It is."

They stood in companionable silence for a while around the Kaa. There was no one else in the room with them and suddenly she was very aware of his presence.

It was like there was some sort of spell being weaved here in this moment, next to the water and with the incense thick in the air, and for a moment she thought about kissing him.

It had been a long time since she'd kissed a man and the thought of kissing him here made her pulse race and her body ache with anticipation.

"It's pretty damp in here. Why don't we go find somewhere to have a cup of tea and maybe lunch?" He didn't wait for his answer, but turned and walked down the hall back to the entrance.

Erica followed him.

The spell was broken, for now.

After the temple and that moment in the Kaa, they drove back toward the base. The drizzle was making it impossible really to enjoy anything. Thorne did suggest heading over to the American village, but Erica didn't really feel like shopping.

Half the stuff she could or would buy, she couldn't even wear on a day-to-day basis anyway. She was either in scrubs working in the hospital, in fatigues or in dress uniform when she was on duty and that was what she was most comfortable in. It was no big loss.

Shopping had always been a luxury in her youth.

With her mother on a widow's pension, there hadn't been much money to go around.

After high school she'd gone straight to college and then Annapolis to help pay for her medical career.

Regina, her one close friend on the *Hope,* had always teased her about being tight with her money. When they would go on shore leave she would be the only one who didn't buy a lot of things.

Things were hard to transport.

Things took up space. Erica was a bit minimalist.

So they headed back to the base and found themselves at the Painappurufeisu.

"Isn't it a little early to drink?" Erica teased, though she was really ready for a drink. The ride back to the base had been silent and awkward.

"Scooby runs a full-service pub. He's got the best pizza near the base."

"Really?" Now she was intrigued.

"Do you like pizza?"

Erica shrugged. "It's okay, but then I really don't have a lot of experience with pizza besides the offerings of chain restaurants. The *Hope* didn't sail in the Mediterranean, so I didn't even get to experience any real Italian pizza. I'm not sure that pizza is my thing."

Great. You're rambling about pizza.

Thorne looked at her like she was crazy and she didn't blame him. She was saying the word "pizza" a lot. Instead he surprised her by asking, "How can pizza not be your thing?"

She chuckled. "I don't know?"

"Pizza has to be everyone's thing. Well, in moderation."

She rolled her eyes, but couldn't help but laugh. "I take it pizza is your thing?"

"And beer."

"Right. You have a taste for the local brews."

"They're good. You'd be surprised. They can have more of a kick than some American beers."

"I can give you a kick if you'd like."

He laughed. "No thanks. I'll take my chances with the local brew. So, are you up for trying some of Scooby's pizza?"

"Sure, but I have to tell you that sounds inherently weird and kind of sacrilegious to my childhood."

Thorne laughed. "His real name is Sachiho, but he actually prefers Scooby. Back before we were ever serving in the Navy, a drunk airman couldn't say his name and called him Scooby instead and it stuck."

"Sachiho...what does that mean?"

Thorne shrugged. "No idea. You could ask him. He would be impressed that you knew it."

"Or he'll just answer me, 'no problem'."

Thorne shook his head. "Again. I'm sorry for that little farce."

"Sure you are."

He pulled in front of the Painappurufeisu. Rock music was filtering through the open windows. The neon sign was flashing, letting everyone know the bar was open for business.

"You know, I was hoping you would take me to eat at a local place. Somewhere authentic."

Thorne held open the door to Scooby's. "Trust me, the pizza here is authentic."

"I don't know whether I should be eager or worried about that."

"You'll have to wait and find out."

As soon as they entered the bar Scooby waved at them. "Hey, Captain Wilder and Commander Griffin, it's a pleasure to see you again."

Thorne waved and then led them to one of the bamboo booths, which was upholstered with a jungle theme material. It was then Erica noticed the wall beside their booth was lined with a green shag carpet.

"I think I've fallen into a time warp." She reached out and touched it to make sure that it was really green shag.

"Why's that?"

"This reminds me of Elvis's jungle room at Graceland."

"Have you been to Graceland?"

"Yes. A couple of times. My *mamère* was an Elvis fan." It was only about four hours from her home in Louisiana to Graceland.

"Ah, I like Elvis too," Scooby said, interrupting. "The King of Rock and Roll. I've been to Graceland too. It's where I got the idea for my jungle-themed dining room."

"Well, Elvis lined the ceiling of his jungle room. Why did you line the walls?"

Scooby shrugged. "I wanted to go all out."

"That you did."

"I told Erica that your pizza was the best around these parts," Thorne said.

Scooby beamed with pride. "This is true. Would you like a pizza?"

"Your house special."

Erica's eyes widened in trepidation. She hoped the special didn't have some kind of delicacy she'd never heard of or something like eel or other sea creature that she had no stomach for.

"No problem—and two beers?" Scooby asked.

"Please." Thorne grinned.

Scooby glanced at her. "You look concerned, Commander."

"I'm not a big fan of pizza."

"No problem, Commander. You will be." Scooby nodded and left.

"He's a man of many layers," she remarked. "Elvis, Graceland and pizza?"

Thorne nodded. "Don't forget bowling. He loves bowling. He loves all things American."

"I can see that, but why didn't he move there?"

Thorne leaned across the table, his eyes twinkling. "His wife wouldn't let him."

Erica rolled her eyes, but she couldn't help but laugh, and she couldn't remember the last time she'd let loose like this. This was better than the tense silence, which had fallen between them at the old temple in Ginowan.

"You know, I would really like to go see the Cornerstone of Peace in Itoman one day," she said, but then realized she was somewhat angling for another date when that was the furthest thing from the truth.

Was it?

Even though the drive to Scooby's had been a little tense, when Thorne had put up his walls again, she was enjoying herself.

Besides, maybe she wasn't *exactly* angling for another date, but another outing with her friend, because that was what they were.

That was all they could be.

"It's impressive. I think everyone should see it once in their life."

"Have you been, Thorne?"

"I have. It lists everyone who died during the battle. Civilian, allied forces and axis powers."

"I'd like to see it."

"We can go after lunch if you want."

"S-sure." And their eyes locked across the table. His was face unreadable as they sat there, that tension falling between them again.

"Here we go. Two beers," Scooby said cheerfully, breaking the silence between them as he set down two dark bottles of beer.

"These have Shisa on them." Erica winked at Thorne.

"Ah, you learned about Shisa today, Commander Griffin?" Scooby asked.

"I did. I also learned your name isn't really Scooby but Sachiho."

Scooby grinned. "Aye."

"What does it mean in Ryukyuan?"

"It's not native to Okinawa. It's more common in Japan. My mother was from Japan. But, in answer to your question, it means 'a charitable man'."

"You're very charitable, Scooby," Thorne teased.

Scooby's eyes narrowed. "You're not getting a free lunch out of me again, Captain."

They all laughed.

"I'll go grab the pizza." Scooby hurried away.

"Did this drunk soldier try to get out of a tab and felt that Sachiho maybe didn't suit Scooby at the time?" Erica asked.

"I never thought of that, but I'm not going to ask him."

Scooby returned and set the pizza down in front of them. "Specialty of the house."

Erica breathed a sigh of relief. "The specialty of the house is pineapple?"

Scooby looked confused. "Painappurufeisu means 'pineapple face'. What did you think my specialty would be?"

Erica laughed. "I have no idea, but I have to learn not to trust Captain Wilder."

Thorne took a swig of his beer, amusement in his eyes.

Scooby *tsked*. "Captain Wilder, you should be nicer to your second in command. Don't listen to a word he says, Commander."

"I'll take that to heart, Sachiho. Thank you."

Scooby grinned and left them to eat.

"Is this why this posting was vacant with hardly any applicants? Do you drive your commanding officers away, Captain?"

He smiled. "Possibly."

"Well, I think I'll take Sachiho's advice and not trust you. Unless we're working in the OR."

"Probably best."

"I've never had pineapple on a pizza before," she remarked.

"Well, then, I wasn't totally off base. It is a delicacy and something you've never had before."

They dug into the pizza and Erica really enjoyed it. While they ate they chatted about life on base and about some of the more colorful characters.

When they were done, she leaned against the back of the booth, staring at the green shag carpeting, chuckling to herself.

"What's so funny?" Thorne asked.

"My *mamère* would really like this place. Hawaii was her favorite vacation spot, the second place being Graceland."

"How many times have you been to...where is Graceland, exactly?"

"Memphis, Tennessee."

"Really?" Thorne asked. "I thought that's where Beale Street was—you know, the birthplace of rock 'n' roll, home of the million-dollar quartet, where Cash got his big break."

Erica cocked an eyebrow. "And who do you think was part of that million-dollar quartet? It was Cash, Perkins, Lewis and Presley."

"I only know about Cash," Thorne said. "Cash was awesome."

"Well, Memphis is home to Beale Street and Graceland. Who do you think invented rock 'n' roll?"

Thorne grinned. "You have me there. That would be interesting to see one day, but don't let Scooby know I have any interest in going to Graceland."

"Why?"

"He'll start the slide show."

Erica laughed and then her phone began to vibrate. She glanced down and saw it was from the hospital. When she looked up she could see that Thorne was looking at his phone as well. "Incoming trauma."

"I know," he said. "Accident on trawler."

"We better go."

Thorne nodded. "Agreed."

They slipped out of the booth and he paid Scooby. As they headed outside Erica could hear the choppers bringing the wounded from the trawler out at sea. The chopper was headed straight for the helipad at the hospital. Several vehicles whizzed by as on-call staff raced toward the hospital.

As she opened the door to Thorne's car a large chopper zoomed overhead. It was loud and nearly ripped the door from her hand, it was flying so low and so fast toward the hospital. It reminded her of the chopper which had brought Thorne aboard the *Hope.*

Only this time it wasn't night, they weren't on a ship in the middle of the ocean, which had gone into silent running and it wasn't a covert operation. This was what she was used to, though she couldn't even begin to fathom the kind of emergency, which would've happened on a trawler off the west coast of Okinawa.

"Let's go, Commander."

Erica nodded and climbed in the passenger seat.

"You know," Thorne said as he started the ignition. "I had every intention of taking you to the Cornerstone of Peace today."

"You did?"

He nodded. "I did."

"Well, maybe another day, then."

Thorne nodded. "Another day."

CHAPTER EIGHT

"WHAT HAPPENED?" THORNE asked the nearest nurse as he came out of the locker rooms, his casual attire abandoned for scrubs. Once they'd pulled up to the hospital Erica had left, running ahead into the fray. Thorne couldn't keep up with her and when an emergency like this was called it was all hands on deck.

He grabbed a trauma gown, slipped it over his scrubs and then grabbed gloves.

"There was an explosion on a trawler. It burned a lot of men and then the trawler started to go down. We have some men with hypothermia and water in their lungs."

"Okinawan?"

"Some. Most of the men are Indonesian, but the trawler was registered to several different countries off the east coast of Africa."

Thorne frowned. "They're fishing far from home."

"You said it, not me."

Thorne nodded at the nurse. Maybe the trawler hadn't been fishing exactly and maybe the men had been up to something else. Either way it didn't matter and it was out of his jurisdiction. Right now he had lives to save. He headed out to meet the gurneys as they came in.

It wasn't long before the doors opened and the rescue team wheeled in a burn victim, who was screaming.

"Male, looks to be about twenty. Indonesian, doesn't speak a word of English."

Great. It was going to be tricky to get any kind of history.

"Get me a translator that knows Indonesian here, stat!" Thorne demanded.

"Yes, Captain!" someone in the fray shouted. He didn't know who, but it didn't matter, as long as his order was taken care of. He needed to know if this boy was allergic to anything and he needed to know what had caused his burn.

Was it fire? Was it chemical? These were the questions he needed answered before he could help his patient. He wanted to make sure if it was a chemical burn that any trace of the chemical was washed from his skin.

"I've got it." Thorne grabbed the gurney and wheeled it to an open triage area. "Don't worry, I'm a doctor, and you're in good hands."

The young man just whimpered, his brown eyes wide with fear and pain. It was obvious that the boy was in shock by his pale complexion, his shaking and his shallow breathing. Thorne slipped nose cannula into his nose.

The boy started to freak out, but Thorne tried to calm him down.

"Breathe, just breathe. It's oxygen."

The boy began to shake, but his breathing regulated as he inhaled the oxygen.

"We need to start a central line." A nurse handed Thorne a tray and he moved into action. The boy reached out and gripped his arm. His eyes were wild as he watched Thorne in trepidation. "I'm sorry, this will hurt—but only for a moment and then it will help."

The boy shook his head, not understanding. He took one look at the needle and started to cry out in fear.

"I need that translator now!" Thorne barked.

"I'm here. I can help." Erica stood in the doorway.

"You know Indonesian?"

"I know a few languages and we helped out in Indonesia quite a lot when I was on the *Hope.*"

"Good. Could you tell him that this will help with the pain?"

Erica nodded and leaned over the patient. *"Hal ini akan membantu."*

"Ask him what kind of burn he has."

Erica asked the boy how he'd got his burns.

"Api."

"Fire, Captain."

"Okay. Then we know how we can proceed. Tell him we'll help him, that this will ease his pain and we'll take care of him."

Erica gently spoke to him. The boy nodded and calmed down. Erica continued to hold his hand.

Thorne inserted the central line as Erica continued to murmur words of encouragement to the frightened boy. Soon he was able to feed the boy medication to manage the pain and the grip on Erica's hand lessened until she was able to let it go.

"You should go back out and lend a hand."

Erica nodded but, the moment she tried to leave, the boy reached out and grabbed her.

"Silakan tinggal."

"What's he saying?" Thorne asked.

"He wants me to stay with him."

"We have other trauma."

"And other surgeons. I can stay for a while. At least until he passes out. He's scared."

Thorne frowned. "I understand your compassion, but this boy's burn will require hours of debridement. Your presence as my second in command is required on the floor."

"I'm sorry, Captain. I have to stay here."

"Are you disobeying me, Commander?"

Erica's eyes narrowed and he could tell she was angry. Heck, he was too. He wished he had the luxury of keeping her in the same room as him as he did his work, but he needed her out there helping, not catering to this boy.

Bunny poked her head into the triage room. "The translator showed up."

"Thanks, Bunny." Thorne turned to Erica. "The translator is here. Go back to the floor, Commander."

Erica bent over and whispered some words to the boy, who nodded and let go of his hold on her. Once he did that Erica moved out of the triage room without so much as a backward glance at him.

Thorne didn't want to annoy her, far from it, but she was a valuable asset to the trauma floor. He couldn't have her playing translator to a scared young man.

"Captain Wilder?"

Thorne glanced up to see a young lieutenant standing in the doorway. "You the translator?"

"Aye, Captain."

"Good. I need to explain what I'm doing to this young man and reassure him that this will help. Nurse, will you gown our translator?"

"Of course, Captain."

Thorne turned back to his instruments while the nurse put a gown and mask on the translator. He glanced out into the trauma floor and saw Erica assessing another patient who had just been brought in. The paramedics had been working on him, giving him CPR as they wheeled him through the hospital doors.

Only now Erica had taken over, shouting orders as she climbed on the gurney to administer CPR, nurses and intern surgeons racing to wheel her away from the oncoming traffic and to a triage room.

Thorne knew he'd made the right decision booting her out of the room. She was a surgeon and a damn fine one.

One that he was proud to have on his team.

Erica stretched. It felt like her back was going to shatter into a million pieces and her feet were no longer useful appendages that she sometimes liked to apply the occasional coat of red nail polish to. No, they now were two lumps of ache and sweat.

"How long was that surgery?" she muttered under her breath as she scrubbed out because she'd lost track of time in there.

"Eight hours," a scrub nurse said through a yawn. "Good work in there, Commander." The nurse left the scrub room and Erica stretched again.

Yeah, she'd believe eight hours for sure, though it felt like maybe that surgery had lasted days. There were a few times she hadn't been sure if her patient was going to make it. She placed her scrub cap in the laundry bin and headed to her locker.

"I heard you had a piece of the trawler's engine embedded in your patient's abdomen?"

Erica groaned, recognizing Thorne's voice behind her. She'd been angry with him for forcing her away, for not letting her comfort that young man, but Thorne had been right.

She needed to be out on the trauma floor, practicing medicine and not translating. If she'd disobeyed orders she wouldn't have been able to operate on her patient and save his life. Her back might've liked that, and definitely her feet, but she was glad she was in the OR doing what she loved.

Saving a life.

Damn. He was right and he probably wasn't going to let her live it down.

"Yes. Part of the engine decided my patient was a good resting place."

Thorne winced. "The prognosis?"

"So far so good. He's in the ICU. How's your patient?"

"Resting comfortably in the burn unit. From what he was telling the translator, that trawler was not fishing off the coast of Okinawa."

"I thought as much."

Thorne crossed his arms. "What made you think that?"

"There were traces of methamphetamine in my patient's blood stream. We had a few close calls on the OR table. A few codes."

Thorne nodded. "The proper authorities have been called. Since they weren't in international waters, we've called the Japanese officials. I'm sure several patients will be interrogated."

"I wouldn't doubt it."

Thorne hesitated, as if he wanted to say more, but couldn't.

Or wouldn't.

Though she barely knew him, Erica recognized a stubborn soul. Sometimes it was like looking in a mirror, because she was stubborn too. Stubborn to the point it had almost cost her her commission a few times.

"You did good in there, Commander."

Erica nodded. "Thank you, Captain."

"Go rest." Thorne turned to leave, but then stopped. "I heard the *Hope* will be in port in a week."

"Really?" she asked.

"Does that make you happy?" he asked.

"It does bring some cheer. Yes. It'll be good to catch up with some old friends."

A strange look passed over his face. "I thought you didn't make friends. I thought you were something of a lone wolf. Like me."

"I had a select few on the *Hope.* It's hard to be confined in close quarters and not make friends, Captain."

"You're right." Then he turned to leave.

"What about our rain check?" she asked, not really believing that she'd asked that. "The Cornerstone of Peace?"

He glanced over his shoulder briefly. "Maybe some other time."

And with that he walked away. He never once brought up her insubordination to her. How she'd almost disobeyed his orders in that triage room. Nor did he apologize for ordering her out. Not that he had to. Captains rarely apologized.

Especially when they were right, and he'd been right.

She'd been the fool. The one in the wrong. And it had probably cost her the friendship.

And more.

Erica closed her eyes and took a deep, steadying breath before turning and heading back toward the locker room. Really, she should be glad that it was such a quick break. That nothing awkward had come between them, which would make it impossible to work with him and would result in her eventual transfer.

This was better.

A working relationship. That was all she wanted from him. He was her commanding officer and she'd do her duty right by him, this hospital and her country.

Still, it stung when he walked away from her and she hated herself a bit for that because, despite every lie she told herself, she really enjoyed their day together.

She liked being around him.

For that one brief moment, it was nice to have a friend.

It was nice to go on a date.

CHAPTER NINE

SHE DIDN'T KNOW he was watching her and Thorne didn't really know why he was watching her. From the research room, he could see out onto the trauma floor. After the trawler accident he'd put her back on some night shifts just so he could get some space from her.

With the *Hope* coming into port, well, it reminded him of when she'd taken his leg. It reminded him of his pain, of his vulnerability, and that she had seen him so exposed.

It was an easy way out, but he hadn't seen her in a week.

Erica had the next two days off while the *Hope* was docked in port.

Still, he didn't know why he remained after hours to do research.

So you could see her. Who are you kidding? He liked to torture himself, apparently.

The research room had a one-way window. You could see out, but not in. He'd really intended to catch up on some work, but the trauma floor was quiet tonight and she was spending a lot of time working on charts at the nurses' station. Again he acted irrationally and avoided her. It was easier than dealing with the emotion she was stirring inside him.

He knew that she was breaking down his walls, ones

he'd had up for ten years since Liam had died. He didn't deserve to be happy again. He'd been the foolish one who'd cost his brother his life.

So he hated himself for wanting Erica, for enjoying the time they spent together. He hadn't realized he was so lonely.

Focus.

Thorne tore his gaze from her and returned to his work. There was a knock at the door.

"Come."

The door opened and Captain Dayton of the USNV *Hope* opened the door.

Thorne stood, saluting the other captain. "Captain Dayton, I wasn't expecting you until tomorrow."

"We got in a bit early and I wanted to check in at the hospital and visit with an old colleague of mine."

"Commander Griffin?" Thorne asked.

Captain Dayton smiled. "Yes. She was a formidable surgeon. I took her under my wing, thought of her like a daughter."

Thorne nodded toward the trauma floor. "She's out there charting if you want to speak with her. I'm sure she'll be pleased to see you."

Captain Dayton smiled. "I will. Thank you. And thank you for accommodating some of my nurses and surgeons. It's very important we have this simulation training to keep us up to date. After this we head back to San Diego to get some retrofits and some much-needed shore leave."

"No problem, Captain Dayton. Your staff has free run of facilities here."

"My thanks, Captain Wilder."

"I hope your staff can have a bit of off-time here in Okinawa. There is a lot to offer."

Captain Dayton cocked an eyebrow. "Is that so?"

"Yes. In fact, I know Admiral Greer was planning on

throwing a bit of a social while the *Hope* is in port. Though that's supposed to be a secret."

Captain Dayton laughed. "I'll keep that secret safe. That sounds like fun. Well, after my crew completes their simulation training, I think they'll have earned the right for a bit of rest and relaxation before heading to San Diego. I'm very much looking forward to your simulation course, Captain Wilder."

Captain Dayton extended his hand and Thorne shook it.

"I look forward to presenting it."

"I think I'll go visit with my former prized officer."

Thorne sat back down as Captain Dayton left the research lab and headed over to Erica. He tried to look away, to give them their privacy, but he couldn't. Something compelled him to watch.

When Erica saw Captain Dayton her face lit up as she saluted him and then embraced him, kissing his cheek. A surge of jealousy flared deep inside him as he watched Erica being so intimate with another man. His jealousy was misplaced. He had no right to feel this way.

He had no claim.

Erica wasn't his.

She could be.

He cursed under his breath and turned back to the computer, but his curiosity got the better of him. Even though he knew he should keep away from Erica, he couldn't help himself.

Despite the warnings he watched the interplay between the two. Captain Dayton was old enough to be Erica's father, but what did that matter? Age was meaningless.

As she talked to her former commanding officer Thorne saw her eyes twinkle. Her smile was genuine and as they talked she reached out and touched him.

When Thorne and Erica talked there was no touching.

When they were together it often felt tense at best because Thorne was too busy trying to keep Erica out.

Thorne sighed. His leg was aching. It was time to get back home, have something to eat, a shower and then bed.

He didn't have time to worry about Commander Griffin. There wasn't enough emotion in him to invest in her.

At least, that was what he kept trying to tell himself.

He went to log off when the door to the research lab opened again.

"Captain! I'm sorry I didn't know you were in here." Erica's face flushed pink, but only for a moment.

"I was just leaving for the night, Commander."

She nodded and stepped into the room, shutting the door behind her. "Are you prepping your simulation for the crew of the *Hope*?"

"I am. It's how to deal with some common medical issues and emergencies Special Ops have to face. Wounds… infections."

Erica sat down at the computer next to him. "Infections like yours?"

"And more. Communicable diseases as well."

"Sounds like a potpourri of fun that you have planned."

He chuckled. "I try my best. I see Captain Dayton found you."

"Yes," she said quickly. "He was a good commanding officer, but a bit suffocating."

Now he was intrigued. "Suffocating? You looked pleased to see him."

"Were you watching me?"

"For a moment."

"For someone who has been ignoring me the last week and giving me endless night shifts again, you're very observant about who I associate with."

"Is this how you usually talk to your commanding officer?"

"No." She grinned. "Just you."

He rolled his eyes. "Thanks. I do appreciate that, Commander Griffin."

"So, you wanted to know how he suffocated me— well, he wouldn't let me do anything without clearing it with him first. At least, for the first year I served under him."

"Everything?"

"Everything. I have to say it's a nice change being under your command, Captain."

"Why's that?" he asked, secretly pleased to hear it.

"You let me do my work."

"I expect nothing less from members of my surgical trauma team. I pick the best of the best."

She blushed. "And I'm the best?"

"One of." He had to get out of here. When he'd moved Erica to some night shifts it was to get some distance between the two of them. This was not distancing himself from her, but Erica had this way of drawing him in.

He both loved and hated that.

"I better go. My shift ended hours ago." He stood. "Have a good night, Commander."

"Thank you, Captain."

Erica had seen many men turn tail and run from an uncomfortable social situation. Usually she thought it looked a bit ridiculous. So much so that it amused her. But this actually made her feel a bit of hope again.

Hope that maybe Thorne hadn't completely washed his hands of her. That maybe, just maybe, he would tear down his walls to let her in.

You're not tearing down any walls.

Which was true.

She wasn't exactly an open book either.

Scooby had called them both stubborn and thought that

Thorne and her together would be volatile. She thought maybe Scooby was right in this instance.

Still, she was drawn to him.

She was attracted to him.

She wanted him.

Get a grip on yourself.

She couldn't want him. She couldn't have him.

Keep lying to yourself.

Erica didn't know he was still in the hospital. She'd come in early to see if she could catch a glimpse of him, but he'd stayed holed up in his office for the entire week. She had heard from some of the nurses that he was dealing with the aftermath of the trawler explosion with the authorities as well as protecting those who were on board the ship and were innocent.

Like the burn victim, Drajat.

He was only eighteen and had had no idea that his uncle, the patient Erica had saved who'd had part of the engine in his abdomen, was drug running.

Drajat had told the authorities that he thought they were actually on a fishing trip. He thought he was earning money so he could attend school; the trace amount of methamphetamines in his system was equal to that of an innocent bystander being around the drugs, but not using them.

Meth was easily absorbed into the skin.

As soon as Drajat was stable enough he would be flown back to Jakarta.

As for Drajat's uncle… He was progressing well, but was still in ICU. Once he was able to be interrogated, well, Erica wasn't sure what the Okinawan police would do with him. This was an international issue as the trawler had crossed into Japanese waters.

"Commander?"

Erica turned in the swivel chair to see that Thorne had returned.

"Yes, Captain? Is there something I can help you with?"

He opened his mouth but then shook his head. "No. It's nothing."

"It's obviously something. I thought you were leaving for the night."

Thorne scrubbed his hand over his face. He looked tired and she didn't blame him in the least. There was also pain behind those eyes. His whole body was clenched tight, taut like a bowstring. It was the leg again.

"I'm sorry for bothering you, Commander. It's nothing." He turned to leave, but hissed through his teeth and reached down.

The last time she'd seen him suffering like this had been when she'd first arrived at the base. When she'd tried to help him he'd bit back at her, lashing out in anger and humiliation.

"You're in pain."

"I've been here too long. It's nothing."

"It's not nothing." She stood and went to the research lab door. Locked it.

"What're you doing?" he asked.

"You're going to sit down and I'm going to massage your leg."

"I don't think so," Thorne snapped. "That's highly inappropriate."

"Do you have a massage therapist who does it for you? Or how about physical therapy?"

Thorne glared at her. "I don't need either. I've been managing well with this prosthesis for some time now."

Erica rolled her eyes. "Sit down, Captain, and that's an order."

"You're ordering me now?"

She crossed her arms. "I am. You should have weekly

massage therapy or physio appointments for your leg. It might have been five years since you lost it, but a prosthetic leg can be hard on the muscle. It's painful."

"I know it is," he growled.

"Thorne, I can help relieve some of your pain. You can barely move, so I can't even begin to imagine how you'll get back home."

She stared him down.

With a grunt of resignation he sat down in an office chair. "So how are you going to help me? Are you going to give me a shot of morphine or some other analgesics?"

"No, I'm going to massage you myself." She slipped off her lab coat and set her phone down on the counter with her stethoscope.

"You're...what?"

"I'm going to massage you. Drop your pants, Captain Wilder."

CHAPTER TEN

THERE HAD BEEN many times since he'd first met Erica when he'd pictured her telling him to drop his pants and in all those scenarios it involved her in a bed, underneath him.

Not once had he ever fantasized about being locked in the research lab, in pain and having her ordering him to take his pants off so she could rub his stump. This was not perfection at all. This was far from it. He didn't want her seeing him like this.

In pain.

Exposed.

"I don't think I heard you correctly, Commander Griffin. You want me to take off my pants?"

She nodded. "Yes. You're wearing suit trousers; it'll be impossible to roll up the leg of said trousers over your prosthetic. Besides, you need to remove your prosthetic so I can massage where it hurts."

"I don't think that's appropriate." He tried to move away, but she blocked him.

"With all due respect, Captain Wilder, I've seen that leg before. I know that leg. I know what was done to it and I know how to relieve your pain."

Though he didn't want to, Thorne took a deep breath and then stood, unbuckling his pants and slipping them off. He tried not to let it bug him that she was seeing him like this: vulnerable. He didn't let any woman see him with his pants off. He didn't let any woman see him with just his prosthetic, let alone the remains of his leg.

Erica did have a point, though. She was the one who'd performed the surgery. She was the one who'd removed his leg, fashioned the stump which had left minimal scarring and a good socket to work a prosthetic in.

The surgeon side of him knew it was a damn good amputation.

The other side of him saw it was a fault. An imperfection. The absence of his leg reminded him that a piece of him was missing and how was that desirable to any woman?

What does it matter? She's off-limits.

And that was why he did as she asked.

He sat down and unhooked the prosthetic, embarrassed that she was there. Their eyes met as she knelt down in front of him, helping him remove the prosthetic and the wrappings underneath, which helped prevent the chaffing.

Her touch was gentle as she ran her hand over his thigh. The simple touch made him grit his teeth as he held back the intense pleasure he was feeling. Her hands on him made his blood burn with need.

It had been so long since he'd been with a woman, but this was not how he'd pictured it. Not even close. The way he fantasized about Erica had nothing to do with his stump, of massaging the knots out of his muscles.

"It healed nicely," she remarked, which kind of shattered the illusion.

"What?" he asked.

"The wound healed really nice. Barely any visible scarring."

"It did. It was a good job."

"I didn't know. You were taken out of my care hours

after surgery and then I never knew what became of you. You had no name, no record."

Thorne shrugged. "Special Ops."

"I know." Her brow furrowed. "Do you have a lot of chaffing?"

"Only when I work long hours. Lanolin helps."

She nodded. "Good. I'm glad to hear it. Let me know if I hurt you."

"It'll hurt no matter what you do, but I'm sure it will feel good after a while. It always does."

"I thought you didn't get a regular massage?"

"I don't—well, not by someone else. I usually handle it on my own."

Erica glanced up. "You should have someone else do it."

"Don't have time for that." He winced as she touched him.

"Am I hurting you?"

Far from it. He loved her touching him.

"Get on with it," he snapped.

"Just try and relax." She began to rub the muscle in his thigh, which was hard as a rock and tense from the pain.

He let out a string of curses.

"Do you want me to stop?" she asked.

"No. It does feel good."

"Your muscles are so knotted."

He nodded and tried not to think about the fact that Erica was kneeling on the floor between his legs, touching him. If he thought about that, then he wouldn't be able to hide anything from her.

So he focused on the pain, but that made it worse.

"Thorne, are you okay?"

"Fine," he lied.

She deepened the massage and beads of sweat broke across his brow. His mind began to wander to that moment when Tyler had been lying in a pool of dirty water. The bullet had grazed him, but Thorne's leg was on fire.

Still, he was the unit's doctor first and foremost. He'd done his duty to make sure Tyler survived.

"You're bleeding, man," Tyler had said as he'd knelt down to tie a tourniquet around his leg.

"I'm fine," Thorne had said. "It didn't nick the artery. Just a bit of bleeding. It'll be fine."

"It's an open wound in the sewer, Wilder."

"I have antibiotics." Thorne had dug through his first aid kit and pulled out a syringe of morphine and a needle and thread.

"What the heck are you doing, Wilder?" Tyler had asked in trepidation.

"Stitching. We still have to swim out to the sub waiting for us. It's shark-infested water. I'm closing up the open wound now."

"It'll get infected that way."

"It doesn't matter. We'll get back to the submarine and it'll be fine. You'll see, Tyler."

Thorne had injected the painkiller and then threaded the needle...

He relaxed, as the pain from his stump seemed to be dissipating. He looked down at Erica working the muscle in his thigh and rubbing around his socket. It was a firm touch, but soft. Her hands were incredibly soft.

Don't think about that.

"Tell me about the surgery," he demanded.

"What surgery?"

"Mine," he said. "Tell me about it. How bad was the leg?"

"Didn't you read your report?"

"There wasn't a lot of information. So tell me. How bad was it?"

"Bad. I won't lie. Your leg was highly infected."

Thorne nodded. "It went down to the bone?"

"Into the tissue," she said. "You did a good repair job on yourself, but..."

"You don't have to say it. I was trapped in an old sewer system for days. If we had been able to get out of there faster and get back to the sub I wouldn't have lost it. I would've been able to stop the spread of the infection."

"Yes. Most likely you could've."

Silence fell between them. It all came back to that moment. She was the one who'd taken his leg and he'd lost it.

"I don't blame you."

She snorted. "Really?"

"I did maybe at first, just a bit."

"You had some pretty choice words for me when you heard me talking about taking it."

"I was a bit fevered by then. My apologies."

"I'm glad to hear you don't blame me. I was worried you did," she admitted, not looking at him, but he could see the pink rise in her cheeks.

"No. If the roles were reversed, and I was given no choice but to amputate or let you die, I would've done the same."

"Does that help?" she asked gently as her ministrations softened.

"It does."

She smiled. "I can tell. Your muscle isn't so knotted. It's relaxing."

"You're good with your hands," he murmured and then gasped when he realized what he'd said. "Erica...I didn't mean..."

Erica was stifling back a giggle and then he couldn't help but laugh as well. It broke the tension that had fallen between them.

Smooth move.

"Well, I suppose I was due for something like that. I

did order you to take off your pants." She wiped a tear from her eyes and then stood. "I would hate for someone with a key to open that door and see me kneeling between your thighs without your pants on."

"Good point." He reached over and began to put on his prosthetic.

"No, let it breathe for a moment. Wearing your prosthetic for so long without a break is why your muscles were so tense."

"So you want me to sit here in the research lab without pants."

Erica grinned, her eyes twinkling. "For another ten minutes and then you can make yourself respectable and head for home. You need rest."

"You do too."

Her smile wobbled and she ran her fingers through her hair. "I have another eight hours on this shift and somehow during my day off I have to study for your intensive simulation."

"You're attending my simulation? I gave you two days off."

"I'm not missing a chance to train with a former Special Ops Navy SEAL. Especially one who performed first aid on himself in the field."

"That was nothing. That was survival."

"I know."

They smiled at each other. It was nice. He'd forgotten how much he missed being around her. His stupid avoiding tactic had cost him.

"Why don't you find a nice on-call room and crash?"

"I think I'll do that. I'll leave you to put your pants on by yourself."

"One leg at a time... Right—I only have one." He winked at her.

"That's a terrible joke."

"I have more." He grabbed his prosthetic. "Go. Rest. You have to rest while you can when you're doing these long shifts."

"I will, but promise me you'll head for home and do the same. I am your second in command here; I can relieve you of your duty."

"Would you get out of here?"

She smiled, grabbed her things and left. Thorne leaned back in the chair, closing his eyes.

He was relaxed for the first time in a long time. When he'd been at the San Diego hospital recovering in a private ward until he'd been able to be debriefed he'd balked at the idea of physiotherapy and massage therapy.

He was made of tougher mettle than that. He only did what was necessary to survive and any physiotherapist who got in his way didn't last long. When he'd lost his leg, he hadn't wanted anyone touching it. The pain was penance.

Erica was right. He needed more help. He needed someone who knew how to massage an amputee. He needed pain relief that wasn't in the form of a pill.

He needed to learn how to manage his pain.

He wrapped his stump, put on his prosthetic, then pulled on his pants, making sure everything was presentable. When he put weight down on his legs, they ached, but they weren't as bad.

A nice, hot shower and bed would help.

He left the research lab and, as he passed an on-call room, he saw Erica was passed out on a cot. She was lying on her side, with her hands curled up under her head. She looked like an angel.

Heck, she was an angel, and he was the very devil himself, because he wanted to join her. He wanted to curl up beside her, wrap his arms around her and lose himself. Only he didn't deserve happiness. One wrong move had cost him his brother. Since he'd cost his brother a life of happiness, he couldn't have what he'd taken from him.

He was unworthy.

You deserve it. It wasn't your fault.

He ignored that voice.

He shut the door to the on-call room and headed out to his car, trying not to think about her between his legs, her hands on a part of him no one had seen in a very long time. He tried not to think about *her*.

Only, that was foolish.

He was a doomed man.

After her shift Erica showered, changed into some casual, comfortable clothes and headed down to the docks. The white hospital ship could be seen blocks away and she couldn't help but grin when she saw it.

She'd served on the USNV *Hope* for so long it was home to her. It felt like she was going home and as she approached the docks, crew members and staff were filtering down the steps off the ship for a brief shore leave before the simulations started tomorrow.

Erica waited on the other side of the barricade, anxiously scanning the crowd for Regina. Of course, her people-watching was constantly interrupted by other colleagues and former crew members who were happy to see her.

When she'd served her time on the *Hope* she'd flown out of Sydney, Australia. *Hope* had been returning out to sea to start a three-month voyage of the South Seas and aid a tsunami disaster.

She hadn't gotten a chance to give a lot of people a proper goodbye. Including Regina, who was very angry that Erica had left in such a rush, but when you were called by the Home Office there was little chance to say proper farewells. There were no gold watch ceremonies in the Navy. One day you were here, the next you could be reassigned and off somewhere else.

Regina was a nurse, but she wasn't part of the Navy, and didn't quite get all the nuances or strict rules which Erica was bound by.

"Erica!"

Erica turned and saw a short, ebony-haired girl pushing her way through the throng of people toward the barricade.

Erica waved at her friend and waited while the Master of Arms cleared Regina for entrance. It only took a few minutes and then that ball of energy was running toward her and throwing her arms around her.

"Oh, my goodness. I've missed you, you crazy lady," Regina said, shaking Erica slightly. "Why the heck did you have to go and get reassigned, and to Okinawa of all places?"

Erica chuckled. "It's good to see you too, Regina. And for your information I quite like Okinawa Prefecture. It's very laid-back here."

"A Naval base laid-back?" Regina asked in disbelief. "I find that laughable."

"Okay, the base may not be laid-back, but the feeling around the island certainly is. Wait until you meet Scooby. He runs the Pineapple Face."

Regina wrinkled her nose. "Please tell me that's a bar?"

"Yes. It's awesome. It's like something out of old sixties sitcom reruns, and the proprietor Scooby is a huge Elvis fan. Huge."

"Oh, I like him already!" Regina slipped an arm through hers and they walked away from the docks. "So I'm being put up in your quarters, eh?"

"Yes. I hope you don't mind that I made those arrangements."

"Are you kidding me? Of course I don't. My new bunk mate on the *Hope* is a bit loony and she snores. Loudly."

"Sorry to hear that, but I talk in my sleep. You used to complain about that."

"I'd rather hear you spout off about elves, turkeys and whatever other nonsense you're dreaming about than Matilda's snore conversations with herself. It's horrible. I suggested she hit the hospital and the sleep apnea clinic. Seriously, there were a few times I thought she was going to inhale her pillow."

Erica laughed until her sides hurt. "So what else is happening on the ship?"

"Same old same old. There's nothing new to report other than Captain Dayton has a new protégé. His name is Lieutenant Clancy and he's really good-looking."

"How good-looking?" Erica asked, having an inkling where this was going. Regina was married to an officer who worked in San Diego, but just because Regina was married it didn't seem to stop her from scoping out gorgeous guys and potential husbands for Erica.

"It's my hobby," Regina had remarked once.

Regina scanned the crowd and then subtly pointed ahead of them. "There. That's how good-looking he is."

Erica glanced over, trying to be nonchalant. Regina was right; he was handsome. Tall and broad-shouldered from the rigorous training. His officer ranking meant he was probably fresh out of Annapolis: Captain Dayton only picked protégés who came from his alma mater. It also meant that he was most likely a trauma surgeon, as was Captain Dayton.

As she was looking at him, he glanced their way and smiled at her. One of those smiles that made Regina swoon and Erica want to put up her defenses.

"He's coming this way," Regina hissed in Erica's ear, barely containing her excitement.

"Hi, there," he said.

"Lieutenant Clancy, this is my friend, Commander

Erica Griffin." Regina could barely contain her excitement.

Lieutenant Clancy came at attention and saluted. "I'm sorry, Commander. I didn't realize who you were."

"At ease. It's okay, Lieutenant. I'm not wearing my uniform. How would you know?"

Clancy smiled. "Are you assigned to this base, Commander?"

"I am. My previous assignment was the *Hope*."

"Really? So you're the surgeon who Captain Dayton has been gushing over since I arrived on board."

She chuckled. "One and the same."

"He didn't mention how beautiful you were, Commander."

Erica tried not to roll her eyes. She really didn't have time for this kind of come-on. And, no matter how cute the lieutenant was, he was Navy and off-limits. All Naval men were.

Except one.

If Thorne had come up to her and given her that cheesy pickup line she might've fallen for it, but then Thorne would never do anything like that. He had pride—an alpha male through and through.

A hero.

"Well, it was a pleasure to meet you, Lieutenant, but Regina and me have some catching up to do and it's my day off." Erica gripped Regina by the arm and forcibly marched her away from the docks at a quick pace.

"Are you crazy? He's really into you."

"Regina, we've been together for what…five minutes?…and you're already up to your old antics."

Regina laughed and squeezed Erica's arm. "And you love it. Come on, admit it, you've missed me."

Erica chuckled. "I've missed you and possibly your tomfoolery."

"Tomfoolery? Easy there, Shakespeare, or I may start up with my buffoonery or clownery."

They laughed together.

"I have missed you," Erica admitted.

"What's it like on the base?"

"Good. It feels odd to not be at sea. When I was back in San Diego before this assignment it was hard to get my land legs back."

Regina grunted. "I know. Every time I have leave and I'm in San Diego with Rick, for two days I swear I'm walking around like I'm drunk."

"You don't have the best land legs."

"Don't even get me started." Regina glanced around. "It's pretty here, though. How far are we away from mainland Japan?"

"Well, you have to take a twenty-four-hour ferry to get to Kagoshima."

"Wow. That's far. I guess living it up in Tokyo is out of the question."

"Yes. You seriously suck at geography."

Regina stuck out her tongue. "So, what else is interesting about this base? You're holding something back. Something you're not telling me."

"What're you talking about?"

"I know when you're hiding something from me."

"I'm not hiding anything from you." Erica let go of Regina's arm. Damn, she hated that Regina was so intuitive. It was what made her a good nurse; she could always glean that little nugget of information out of a patient. "Are you hungry? I'll take you to that pub I was talking about."

"What are you hiding from me?"

"Nothing! I'm just trying to feed you." Then Erica spied exactly what she was trying to hide. Thorne was walking their way.

Regina had been there, working with Erica when

Thorne had come in. She'd been his nurse for the few brief hours he'd been on board. Of course, he hadn't pleaded with her about his leg; he hadn't reached up and kissed her and called her beautiful.

"Angel."

"Oh, my God!" Regina froze. "Look who it is."

Erica grabbed her and pulled her behind a shrub. "Get down!"

"What?" Regina smiled then. "That's what you're hiding."

"Shut up!"

They crouched behind the bush until Thorne walked past and was out of sight. Erica let out a sigh of relief.

"That's that SEAL from…what…five years ago? The one who you were fighting so hard to keep on the ship. I thought for sure he would've died."

"I thought he did too."

Regina crossed her arms. "So why are we hiding from him, then?"

"We're not."

"Please. What was with the 'get down!' then?"

"I thought I saw a bug." Erica was not the best liar in the world, especially when she tried to lie to Regina; she didn't even know why she bothered with it.

"Please. Since when have you been afraid of bugs? Remember when we stopped in Hong Kong? You were the only one who tried those fried bugs. Which, by the way, still freaks me out to this day."

"There's nothing to tell."

"Who is he?"

"Captain Wilder is my commanding officer," Erica responded. There was no point in hiding that aspect. Regina would find out.

"Does he know?"

Erica shook her head. "I'm not talking about this. I'm going to get something to eat."

"Well, first can I drop my duffel bag off at your quarters?"

"Okay. Then eat."

"Yes. Then eat." Regina rolled her eyes. "In time you'll tell me. You always do."

Not this time, Erica thought to herself. She wasn't saying anything more, because there was nothing to tell. Absolutely nothing.

Except undeniable chemistry.

She cursed silently to herself. It was happening again and she didn't want it to.

Yes, you do.

No. There was nothing secretive or gossip-worthy in nature about her and Thorne. All Regina needed to know was that Thorne was her commanding officer and that he would be running the simulation tomorrow. That was it. End of discussion.

CHAPTER ELEVEN

WHY IS HE TOUCHING HER?

It was ticking him off because he should be focusing on the simulation lab, which was about to start. He'd been collected and ready to start at zero nine hundred hours, until some young lieutenant had come in and sat down next to Erica.

She was smiling at him as they spoke quietly to each other and then the lieutenant put his arm on the back of her chair. He wasn't totally touching her, but it was close enough.

Why should you care?

He shouldn't. He had no prior claim to Erica. She was off-limits. She wasn't his. Though he wanted her. He desired her. There was no use denying it anymore, to himself, at least. That was where those feelings were going to stay, buried deep inside.

Thorne cleared his throat and shuffled his papers, trying to ignore Erica and the lieutenant, but he couldn't.

Just like he hadn't been able to keep his eyes off of her last night at the pub. She'd been laughing and having a good time with a friend from the *Hope*. The lieutenant had been there, joking and smiling with them.

Thorne's only company had been Scooby.

"She doesn't laugh like that with you."

"Thanks for pointing that out, Scooby. I appreciate it."

Scooby had shaken his head. "That's not what I mean. It's all fake."

"I find that hard to believe, Scooby."

"It's fake. When she looks at you, that's something more. It's better."

Though Scooby hadn't been able to elaborate on how it was better.

Thorne found that hard to believe. She didn't look at him *different*. Not that he could tell. Then he uttered a few oaths under his breath, mad at himself for thinking about Erica and thinking about looks and lieutenants.

He glanced at the clock on the wall. It was nine. Time to start.

"Welcome everyone to my simulation lecture today." He moved around the other side of the podium. "Today we're going to be using robotic simulators and your tools would be the general tools that could be used in battle or emergency situations. There will be very basic tools, because in extreme circumstances you have to think with your head and improvise. I will be breaking you off into teams and each team will be given a different scenario."

"How long do we have, Captain?" a young ensign asked.

"I will start the timer. The first team to finish successfully, well, I don't have a prize." He grinned. "But perhaps I can be persuaded."

There was a bit of laughter and his gaze fell on Erica. She was smiling at him warmly. The same way she'd looked at him when they'd had pizza together at Scooby's place and, though he should just ignore it, he couldn't help but return her smile.

Concentrate.

"Okay. Organize yourself into teams. I want a mixture

of levels of command. Not all surgeons with each other. I want to see a true team of medical professionals."

As they organized themselves into teams, he got his cards ready and Erica came up beside him.

"I think your prize should be one of Scooby's house pizzas."

"That might appeal to some, but really, what's so special about a pineapple pizza?"

"That it's one of Scooby's," she said matter-of-factly.

He chuckled. "Well, if I'm offering that, I don't think it's very fair that you're participating in this simulation. You've already had a taste of the prize. It might drive you to cheat."

"Are you calling me a cheater, Captain Wilder?"

"If the shoe fits."

"I'll have you know..." She trailed off and then the joviality disappeared. "Well, I better get to my team."

He watched her walk away, and then turned back to see that friend of hers watching them with a strange look on her face, like she'd caught them doing something naughty. What the heck was happening to his hospital?

Since when had he reverted back to high school? Because that was what it felt like and he was not happy about that.

"Can I help you...?"

"I'm a nurse, Captain." She stepped forward. "My name is Regina Kettle. I'm a nurse on the *Hope.*"

Thorne nodded. "And is there something I can help you with? Do you have a question about the simulation?"

"No, not at all. My apologies for staring, but I think I know you."

So that's why she was staring and why Erica was acting weird. Did this nurse remember him as a patient? Had this nurse seen him when he'd been so vulnerable? That thought made him nervous.

"I don't think so."

She narrowed her eyes. "Well, maybe not, then."

"We're about to get started."

"Sure thing, Captain." She moved past him and returned to her team.

Don't let her shake you.

It didn't matter if she remembered him. It didn't matter if she'd been there when he'd lost his leg. It didn't make him less of a soldier or a surgeon.

Something it had taken him a couple of years to deal with himself when he could no longer be a part of the Special Ops.

So why is it bothering you so much?

He silenced the niggling voice in his head. When he looked over at Erica she was on the lieutenant's team and he was leaning over her, whispering in her ear while they went over what supplies they had.

"Lieutenant!" he snapped.

The lieutenant in question looked up, his cheeks flushing with color. "Yes, Captain Wilder?"

"What's your name, seaman?"

"Lieutenant Jordan Clancy." He saluted.

"Tell you what, I'd like you to switch places with the Ensign Fitz over here. I think the ensign would benefit more from working with Commander Griffin."

The blush remained. "Of course, Captain."

Lieutenant Clancy and Ensign Fitz switched places. Thorne felt a little inkling of satisfaction and then he noticed the nurse was smiling smugly to herself, as if she'd uncovered some kind of secret.

He was not handling this well.

Pathetic.

And he was angry with himself for being so petty. This was what Erica did to him. She made him think and act irrationally. Before she arrived he'd led a relatively quiet existence. He didn't wrestle with his guilt every day.

What existence?

"All right, I'll be handing out your scenarios. Do not look at them until I start the clock." He passed cards to all the teams and then pulled out his timer. "Okay, go!"

The teams began to move quickly, moving through the scenarios and working together with the minimum equipment they had.

There were some promising officers, surgeons and medical personnel training in the simulation today. Erica handled her team efficiently as they dealt with the trauma to the chest wall. She immediately reached for the plastic bag and tape to stop the wound and the patient from bleeding out so they could properly assess them.

It gave him a sense of pride to watch her.

She was incredibly talented, beautiful, poised and a commendable second in command and officer.

And totally off-limits.

At least that was what he kept trying to tell himself, but he wasn't sure if he wholly believed it anymore.

"Are you sad your team lost?"

Erica was startled to see Thorne taking the seat next to her at the bar.

"No, not at all." She took a sip of her drink. "We would've won except for Ensign Fitz's blundering mistake."

"You mean when he killed your patient?" Thorne asked.

She laughed. "Yes. That does put a damper on the contest."

"He needed to learn."

"I could've won had you not taken Lieutenant Clancy from me."

His expression changed just slightly and he shifted in his seat. "Were you mad at my decision?"

"No, other than I lost." She leaned over. "I hate to lose, by the way. Just for future reference."

He smiled and nodded. "Noted."

"So why did you pull the lieutenant from my team?"

"I thought you said you weren't mad," he replied.

"Not mad. Just curious. I want to know what drove you to your decision."

"Ensign Fitz has a lot to learn and you're a damn fine surgeon."

Somehow she didn't believe him. Regina had suggested that Thorne had moved Lieutenant Clancy because he was jealous and possessive at the time. Regina had said she saw the way Thorne looked at her and, the moment Jordan had begun to whisper sweet nothings in her ear, Thorne moved him.

Erica thought the whole thing was preposterous.

Although the "sweet nothings" wasn't totally off; Lieutenant Clancy had been flirting with her, telling her how good she looked and asking her out for a drink later—which Erica had promptly turned down, much to Regina's chagrin.

"It's Captain Wilder, isn't it? You have the hots for him."

"I don't have the hots for him, Regina. I just have no interest in dating a superior or any officer."

Regina had rolled her eyes. "Then who are you going to date?

"No one."

"You're hopeless."

This was why Erica didn't date. Maybe she was hopeless, but there was good reason. Her career was too important.

She would never risk that for anything. Even a stolen moment with Thorne.

"Thank you, Captain. I appreciate the compliment."

"Thorne, remember? We're off duty."

"Right." She began to peel at the label on her domestic beer. The happy-looking squid was starting to lose tentacles as Erica nervously shredded the label, which was soft as the water was condensing on the outside of the bottle.

Don't think of him that way.

"So what did you think of the simulation today?" he asked.

"I thought it was good. Better than some other simulations I'd been involved in. Some are just endless lectures."

"I don't lecture."

She laughed. "I saw you tear down Ensign Fitz when he killed our robotic patient."

"That's a stripping down. It's not a lecture."

"It sounded like one of my father's." She took another swig of beer.

"Your father served, didn't he?"

"He did. He was a good officer, but I'm not like him." She didn't want to talk about her father. Not because she wasn't proud, but because people's condemnation and their scrutiny of her father cut her to the quick.

"How do you mean?"

She shook her head. "I'm not as strong as he was."

"You're just as strong. I see it."

"He wasn't called mentally unstable while he served."

It was only after.

She sighed. "Sorry."

"No, it's okay. I apologize for that. It was uncalled for."

"I'm used to it. It seems wherever I go I'm judged on that. Judged for making one mistake. I've had so many psychiatric evaluations and understanding conversations…"

Thorne held up his hands. "Erica, I was just making conversation. I don't think that at all."

Had she just heard him right?

"You don't?" she asked in disbelief.

"Why would I? Why I would judge you on the mistakes another made? You're a totally different person—I think, perhaps, stronger with all you've had to deal with. Was your father a medical officer?"

"No."

"Well, then, I don't know how you can be held to the same standard as him and vice versa. Serving as a medical officer is totally different than a plain officer."

"And being a Special Ops SEAL is so much more." She reached out and squeezed his hand. "Did you deal with PTSD when you returned home?"

"That's classified." He winked.

"I can always request your medical record as your surgeon."

He leaned over and she felt his hot breath as he murmured in her ear. "You can't. You're not on my record. It was wiped. I have never been on board the *Hope*."

"That's terrible! So who did they say did the surgery, then?"

He shot her a wicked grin. "Me."

"You?"

"Me. I was the medical officer with the unit."

"So you amputated your own leg, in the field in a very neat and dare I say brilliant way?"

His blue eyes twinkled. "You got it."

"You're not serious, are you?"

"Would I lie to you?"

Erica laughed. "Really, we're going to head back into *that* territory, are we?"

Thorne shrugged. "I'm absolutely dead serious. According to my official medical file out of San Diego where

I recuperated, I was the chief medical officer in my unit, and I alone amputated my own leg."

Erica muttered a few choice curses that were quickly drowned out by an inebriated seaman shouting for music.

"No problem!" Scooby got up and selected music on his tiny digital jukebox, blasting a song at an obnoxious level as people crowded the dance floor.

Thorne laughed. "Do you want to dance?"

"Are you insane?"

"No, I'm serious. Come on; this is a fun song."

Erica shook her head in disbelief as a weird, drunken crowd formed on the small dance floor in front of them.

"I can't believe what I'm seeing."

"What, the dance or the crowd?" Thorne teased.

"Both." Erica took a swig of her drink. "I'm surprised that no one is filming this. This is going to end up on the internet."

"Good idea." Scooby scurried away.

Erica gave Thorne a sidelong glance. "You don't think he's going to get a camera, do you?"

"Don't put it past him. He might actually still have a camcorder back there."

Scooby returned and held up his phone. "Come on, Captain Wilder and Commander Griffin. Get out there and dance."

"She said no, Scooby."

Scooby frowned. "Why?"

"I don't dance in such an organized fashion." She winked at Thorne, who was laughing.

"Bah, you're no fun. I'll film you anyway."

"I have to get out of here," Erica shouted over the din. She set the money down on the counter. "Do you want to get out of here, Thorne?"

"What?" he asked, wincing.

"Let's go!" she shouted and took his hand, pulling him

out of the bar. They managed to avoid Scooby's camera by disappearing in the throng of people that was now gathering around the edge of the dance floor.

She hated really thick crowds in small spaces. So it wasn't that she was afraid of dancing, or being caught on Scooby's video and ending up online, she just knew it would be a sudden crush of people and she didn't want to have a panic attack in front of Thorne.

When they were outside Erica took a breath of fresh air and began to laugh. "That was crazy. I didn't think Scooby had that repertoire of music."

"He has all kinds."

"I thought he only liked Elvis?" she asked.

"He's a man of many layers. Like an onion."

They began to walk along the sidewalk. The stars were out and a large full moon was casting an almost near-perfect reflection on the water of the bay. The *Hope* loomed up out of the darkness. The white color of the ship caught the light from the moon and the bridge was lit. She knew Captain Dayton was up on his bridge overseeing some of the minor works before they set back out on the ocean again the day after tomorrow. The major retrofit would happen when they docked in San Diego.

"Do you miss serving on the ship?" he asked, breaking the silence.

"Sometimes," Erica said. "I wanted a change. I like the different opportunities. I'm pretty blessed to do what I love to do."

"I get it."

"Do you miss being a part of Special Ops?" she asked.

He cocked his eyebrows.

"Yeah, I know, a dumb question. Of course you do." She sighed. "It's a beautiful night; do you want to walk down to the beach?"

"No, my leg isn't so good on the sand at the best of times. I don't want to be stumbling at the moment."

She didn't know what he meant by that, but they kept on the main path toward the officers' quarters.

"What do you remember of that day?"

"What day?" she asked.

"I guess I should say *night*, but I'm not really sure if it was night when you took my leg."

"I didn't take your leg, Thorne."

"I know—when you operated," he said, correcting himself.

"I remember everything."

"You do?" he asked, surprised.

"I do. I wondered what happened to you for so long."

"So it was just curiosity about my well-being?"

"No, there was more to it." They stopped in a small green, which was between the hospital, the docks and the officer quarters. Suddenly she was shaking and she didn't know why; she was falling fast and she was so scared about taking the step.

What if I get burned again?

"What else?" He took a step toward her, his hands in his pockets, like he was trying to stop himself from something.

"Your eyes." Then she reached out and lightly touched his face. "You were scared, but I don't think it was fear. It was something else. Your eyes haunted me."

"So my eyes haunted you?"

"You mentioned someone: Liam. Who was he?"

Thorne stiffened at the name. "Someone I knew a while ago."

It was apparent that the topic of Liam was off-limits.

"You said I was as beautiful as an angel." Her cheeks burned with heat; she couldn't look up at him and when she did he ran his thumb over her cheek.

"You are," he whispered. His eyes sparkled in the dark; her pulse was thundering between her ears and her mouth went dry. Thorne's hand slipped around her waist, his hand resting in the small of her back. He was so close, they were so close, and all she wanted him to do was kiss her again.

You're so weak.

She couldn't let this happen again but she wanted it too. She was so lonely.

"Thorne, I don't know... This isn't right."

He took a step back. "You're right. I'm sorry."

"No, don't be sorry. I want to, trust me, but...I can't. I don't have room for anyone in my life but me."

"Neither do I, Erica. I can't promise you anything."

"I don't need promises. I've had promises made before and they were always broken. I don't rely on them." This time she was the one who closed the distance between them. "I don't expect any promises."

"Then what do you want?" he asked as he ran his knuckles down her cheek.

She wasn't sure what she wanted. She wanted to be with Thorne in this moment, but what would it do to her reputation? Could she just have one night with him?

That was what she wanted.

Just one night of passion.

Perhaps, if she fed the craving she had for him, then it would burn him from her system and she could move on. It would clear the air.

You're weak.

"What do you want, Erica?" His voice was husky as he whispered the words into her ear.

"I want you to kiss me." She reached out and gripped his shirt.

He leaned forward and she closed her eyes as he kissed her. And then it deepened and she was lost.

CHAPTER TWELVE

ERICA WASN'T SURE how they got to Thorne's door. All she knew at that moment was she had him pressed against the door, was melting into him. His kiss made her weak in the knees, senseless, and she didn't want it to end.

He gently pushed her away and she moaned.

"What?" she asked.

"I have to open the door," Thorne answered, his voice husky with promise.

"Good; I thought you'd changed your mind."

"No, never." And then he pulled her into another kiss, which seared her blood and made her swoon against him.

"Open the door." Erica let him go for just a moment as he unlocked the door. Once it was open he scooped her up, causing her to shriek.

"What're you doing?"

He shut the door behind him with a kick from his right leg. "Carrying you to my bedroom."

"You can't."

Thorne kissed her. "Watch me."

And he did carry her to his bedroom, then set her down on her feet. She slowly slid down the length of his body, feeling the heat of him through seemingly many layers of his clothes. Clothes she wanted gone as soon as possible.

"You look good enough to eat," he whispered against her neck.

Her pulse quickened. "Pardon?"

"You heard me. I've been fighting it all evening. Seeing you in the bar by yourself... I've been fighting the urge to take you in my arms from the moment you landed in Okinawa."

"Tell me more."

Thorne moaned and held her tighter. Her body was flush with his and Erica wanted the layers separating them to be gone. She wanted them to be naked, skin to skin.

"Do you want me to tell you or do you want me to show you?"

Erica didn't respond to that, instead she used her mouth to show him exactly how much she wanted from him. She was tired of being alone and for once she wanted to feel passion again, even if it was only fleeting. Thorne was worth it.

The room was dark except for a thin beam of light through the curtains and she was aware how close they were to Thorne's bed. She was suddenly very nervous. It had been so long since she'd been with a man. It felt like the first time again.

"What's wrong?" Thorne asked, brushing her hair from her face. "Are you having second thoughts?"

"No. No, I'm not having second thoughts. It's just been a long time since I've been with a man."

"It's been a long time for me too."

"I want you, Thorne. All of you." And she wanted it. She wanted him to possess her. For once she didn't want to be the woman men were afraid of because of her rank and her training. Tonight she was just Erica. She was just a woman and he was a man.

He kissed her again, a featherlight one, then buried his face against her neck. His breath caressed her skin, making goose pimples break out. A tingle raced down her spine and she sighed. She couldn't help herself.

"Take off my clothes," he whispered.

Erica did just that. Unbuttoning his shirt and running her hands over his chest, it was mostly bare except for a bit of hair, which disappeared under the waist of his pants. Next she undid his belt, pulling it out and snapping it. He slid his hands down her back and cupped her butt, giving her cheeks a squeeze.

"Don't be naughty," he teased.

"I swear I won't." And then she undid his pants, crouching to pull them down. He kicked them off and then moved to the bed, sitting down to remove his prosthetic leg. "Let me."

His body stiffened as she ran her hands over his thigh again and undid his prosthesis, setting it against the nightstand. She started to massage his thigh; he moaned.

"That feels good, but I don't want you to massage me," he said.

"Oh, no."

"No." He pulled her close, kissing her. "Now it's your turn. Undress."

Erica stood and began to take off her clothes. His eyes on her excited her, making her heart race. She'd never done anything like this before. It was usually lights-out, under the covers. She'd never stripped for a man before.

"You're so beautiful. Like an angel," he murmured. He reached out and pulled her down to him. "So beautiful."

"Thorne..." She trailed off because she didn't know what else to say to him. His hands slipped down her back, the heat from his skin searing her flesh and making her body ache with need. She was so exposed to him; it thrilled her. She'd never felt like this before. He cupped her breasts, kneading them, and she moaned at the sensation of his hands on her sensitized skin.

He pinned her against the mattress, his lips on hers, their bodies free of clothing and skin to skin.

She was so ready for him. Each time his fingers skimmed her flesh her body ignited. He pressed his lips against her breast, laving her nipple with his hot tongue. She arched her back. She wanted more from him. So much more.

Erica wanted Thorne to make her burn. To make her forget everyone else. His hand moved down her body, between her legs. He began to stroke her, making her wet with need.

"I want you so bad."

Erica moaned as he moved away and pulled a condom out of his nightstand drawer.

Thorne moved back to her. "Now, where were we?"

He pressed her against the pillows and settled between her thighs. He shifted position so he was comfortable. The tip of his sex pressed against her. She wanted him to take her, to be his.

Even though she couldn't be.

Thorne thrust quickly, filling her completely. She clawed at his shoulders, dragging her nails down his skin as he stretched her. He remained still, but she urged him by rocking her hips. She wanted him to move. To take her.

"You feel so good." Thorne surged forward and she met every one of his thrusts.

She cried out as he moved harder, faster, and a coil of heat unfurled deep within her. Then it came, pleasure like she'd never experienced before. It flooded through her and overwhelmed her senses, her muscles tightening around him as she came. Thorne's thrusts became shallow and he soon joined her in his climax.

His lips brushed her neck as she held him against her and then he rolled onto his back, pulling her with him, so she could hear his heart beating. She lightly ran her fingers across his skin while his own fingers stroked her back.

"I'm sorry that was so fast. I needed you so bad, I couldn't hold back."

"It was amazing," she whispered. "No apology necessary."

Erica settled against him, the only sound was that of the ocean outside and his breathing and then she tensed as she realized what she'd done. She'd fallen in with another commanding officer, something she'd sworn she'd never do again. As the euphoria melted away, she was angry at herself for being so weak.

How could she have let this happen again?

Thorne isn't like Captain Seaton. You didn't make any promises.

Captain Seaton had been angry that she'd been the one to reject him ultimately and that was why he tried to ruin her career.

She didn't think Thorne was like that. He seemed to have a good head on his shoulders. He was rational, but a bit of niggling self-doubt ate away at her. Trust was a big issue for her. She wasn't sure if she could trust Thorne.

She wasn't sure if she would honestly trust another man again.

Thorne watched her. He wasn't sure if she was sleeping. Her eyes were closed, but her breathing wasn't deep, as if she was in sleep. He knew he'd promised her that nothing had to happen out of this, that was the way she wanted it and that was what he wanted. Wasn't it?

Of course that was what he wanted.

They'd made no promises; if promises had been exchanged he wouldn't have gone through with it, because he was never going to have a relationship. He'd been weak and forgotten that he couldn't have her.

He rolled over onto his back and scrubbed his hands over his face, staring up at the fan slowly rotating on his ceiling. What had he done? The guilt ate at him.

"What's wrong?" Erica murmured.

"Nothing." He turned to his side again. "Just watching you sleep."

"Why are you watching me?" she asked, moving onto her side and tucking her hands under her head.

"I couldn't help it. It was relaxing."

"That groan you gave out didn't sound like you were at ease."

"Perhaps not."

She smiled and then frowned. "So, what happens now?"

"What do you mean?"

"I mean when we're back on duty." Erica leaned on an elbow. "I don't want any awkwardness. I'd like to act like nothing happened between us."

"We'll just go on as normal. Nothing has to change; I think we both made our intentions clear."

"We did." Then she got up, holding the sheet against her.

"Where are you going?"

"Back to my quarters." She bent over, picking up the pieces of her clothing scattered all around the room.

"I'm not kicking you out, Erica. You don't have to leave."

"I do." She sat down on the edge of the bed and began to dress. "If I stay, then it might mean more."

"I won't think that. Come back to bed."

Erica chuckled. "Is that your best 'come hither' look?"

"I wasn't aware I was doing one." He leaned across and pulled her back down against the mattress to place a kiss on her lips upside down. "Stay."

"I can't. Remember, I have Regina staying with me. If

I don't come back to bed, she's going to wonder and then start poking around. She might even get a transfer until she figures it all out."

Thorne shuddered. "Okay, you better go, but know this—it's against doctor's orders."

She rolled her eyes, got up and finished dressing. Then she came around to his side of the bed and kissed him.

"Thanks for tonight."

"Anytime." He wanted to say more things. He wanted to tie her down in his bed and never let her go, but she was right. If she came out of his quarters the next morning and someone saw her, there would be gossip. She didn't want any more gossip about her, which was fair.

He didn't want the gossip either. Thorne didn't want to get her in trouble or transferred. Losing her would be detrimental to the welfare of the base hospital.

And you too.

Yeah, he'd miss the comraderie. She was the only second in command he'd ever met who'd stood up to their commanding officer. Who worked alongside him as a team. They were equals.

She was strong.

Thorne had thought being with her once would flush her from his system, instead he found himself wanting more.

So much more.

Erica tried to sneak back into her quarters. The television had been flickering in the window when she approached and she was worried that as soon as she walked through the door she'd be bombarded with questions, but when she peered through the window she could see that Regina was passed out in front of the TV.

Maybe dancing at Scooby's had exhausted her.

One could only hope.

Erica shut the door behind her as quietly as she could, locked it and then slid off her shoes to creep along the tiled hallway to her bedroom.

She was almost home free.

"Where were you tonight?"

Darn.

Erica turned to see Regina sitting upright, no sign of being asleep or having been asleep. "You were awake when I came home, weren't you?"

"I was. I saw you peek through the window."

"You're a pain." Erica tried to escape again, but she was up against a pro.

"Where were you?"

"I'm an adult. You're not my mother."

Regina crossed her arms. "I was worried when you disappeared from the bar. It would've been nice if you had told me where you were going."

"You're so good at guilt."

A small smile played around Regina's lips. "I'm sorry, but it's true. I was worried."

"You were worried? You were too busy dancing." Erica mimicked Regina's terrible but endearing moves.

Regina rolled her eyes. "Come on. I don't get out much."

"It's apparent."

"I still don't know how that song started."

"Some poor seamen who had had too much to drink." Erica set her purse down on the counter in her kitchen and went to get a glass of water. Regina laughed. "And why didn't you jump in?"

"Oh, I was in the middle of talking to Thorne." And then she cursed under her breath, realizing she'd said "Thorne" to Regina instead of calling him Captain Wilder. Dang.

"Who?"

"Captain Wilder."

"So we're on a first-name basis with Captain Wilder, now, eh?"

"Shut up." Erica took a big swig of water, trying to ignore Regina who was smugly dancing around the kitchen.

"I knew it. I knew something was up. You were with him, right?"

"Yes."

"You are such a bad liar!" Regina exclaimed. "I so *knew* you two had chemistry floating around. Why else would you dive behind a bush to avoid someone? You've never hid from anyone or anything before. Tell me everything!"

"There's nothing to tell."

Liar.

There was a lot to tell, but it was stuff she wasn't sure she wanted to share at this moment because she wasn't exactly sure of how she was feeling herself. When she'd come here and seen that her commanding officer was Thorne, she'd been worried that she would be too weak to resist him. She didn't want another relationship. That was what she kept telling herself. It became a broken record in her head.

And, just like any song you heard over and over, the broken record had become nothing more than background noise when Thorne took her in his arms and kissed her. Now she didn't know what to do with all these emotions swirling around inside.

She was torn and frightened.

"Come on, there has to be something going on. You're sneaking into the house in the middle of the night." Regina looked her up and down. "You reek of guilt."

Erica rolled her eyes. "How can I reek of guilt?"

Regina leaned forward and sniffed. "Okay, not guilt,

but cologne or something very manly. Unless you've taken to wearing men's deodorant."

"You know what? I have." Erica set the glass in the sink. "I'm kind of tired. I think I'm going to hit the hay. I have a long duty-shift tomorrow."

"Erica, it's okay to admit you like this guy."

"No, it's not. You know my story. You know what happened to me before. I was in a relationship with my commanding officer before the *Hope,* and I thought he loved me, but he didn't. Not the way I loved him and so I broke it off. I was the one that was isolated. I was the one who was getting the crummy shifts. I was the one passed up for commendation and promotions. I was the one he reported as mentally unstable. It's why I left."

"I thought you didn't want a relationship because of your mom losing your dad."

Erica sighed and leaned against the counter. "That's part of it, but not really. I saw what my father's service did to his marriage and his family, but that didn't stop me from serving. That didn't stop me from proving to everyone that I was a good officer too. I stepped out of my father's shadow long before my relationship with Captain Seaton."

Regina nodded. "Okay, so your holdup is not your parents' marriage, but being burned by a lover?"

"I guess so. See, before I was hurt I thought my perfect match would be someone who served in the same capacity as me. My mother was not in the Armed Forces."

"Erica, you had one bad relationship. Who doesn't?"

"Has a former lover almost ruined your reputation and career by calling you mentally unstable?"

Regina bit her lip. "Well, no."

"Then you're not an authority."

"Look, we've all been hurt by love before we found that perfect someone. I think that Thorne is your perfect someone."

"And how would you know that? You've met him once."

Regina shrugged her shoulders. "I just know. I'm quite intuitive and you've said that countless times. I have it on record."

Erica chuckled. "Intuitive in your job."

"Well, it counts for knowing good relationships too."

"There's no relationship. He doesn't want one either."

"How do you know?"

"He told me."

Regina frowned and pursed her lips together. "I don't buy that. I think you should talk to him about your feelings."

"What feelings?" She would have got away with that except she blushed. There were feelings there; she just wasn't sure she was ready to admit those feelings. Not yet.

When?

And that was the conundrum she was in. She was being a coward and she hated that. Erica wasn't a coward.

"I don't know why you're trying to deny them." Regina sighed. "Whatever you do, you have to tell him."

"I'm telling you, he doesn't want anything more than what we had tonight, Regina."

"Do you know that with one-hundred-percent certainty?"

No, she couldn't. She really didn't know how Thorne was feeling. Maybe he'd just been saying those things to get her between the sheets, maybe not. Damn it, she didn't have time for this. A relationship was not on the cards for her.

She wasn't going to put her heart on the line again.

Career was all that mattered. She just wanted to keep advancing until she commanded a posting of her own.

Relationships, love, family: they just tied you down.

You're lonely.

Lonely or not, it wasn't an excuse to go out and just

marry the first guy you came across so you could get those two kids you'd secretly been longing for, which would put a strain on the marriage, which would eventually result in divorce because that significant other didn't get your passion, your drive.

Her head began to pound.

"I'm going to bed. Good night, Regina." Erica turned to leave, but Regina stopped her. "Regina, I'm really tired."

"I know. Look, I'm sorry." Regina gave her a hug. "I just want you to be happy. I saw the way you two looked at each other, and I think it's mutual, but until one of you opens up nothing is going to happen. I know you don't want to hear it, but I think you two are perfect for each other."

I think so too.

"I can't open up, Regina. I just can't." She gave her friend another hug. "I'm going to get some sleep. Should I wake you to say goodbye before I go to work?"

"Yes," Regina said. "Or I'll kick your butt."

Erica grinned. "Just think, in a few days you'll be on a leave with Rick in San Diego."

"Not just a leave."

"Oh?"

"I'm going to take a job at a private clinic in San Diego. Rick and I are trying."

"For a baby?" Erica asked surprised.

"Yep."

"So you won't be going back on the *Hope*?"

Regina shook her head. "Nope. This was my last run."

"So that's why you're trying to fix me up. You're trying to make sure I'm taken care of before you head for the public sector."

"You got it. I will succeed."

"Keep thinking that."

"I'm glad I got to see you. Perhaps Rick will get stationed in Okinawa. If not, I'll come visit."

"You better."

Regina smiled. "Go sleep. I'll see you tomorrow."

Erica nodded and took herself off to bed, but she doubted she'd get any sleep, and she was right. As soon as her head hit the pillow, she rolled over on her right and stared at the empty spot beside her.

The emptiness had never bothered her before, but now it did. She was very aware how empty her bed was and she was mad at herself for caring.

She was mad at herself for wanting something she knew she couldn't have.

CHAPTER THIRTEEN

"GOOD MORNING," THORNE WHISPERED, his breath fanning against her neck. She didn't even hear him come up behind her. She was busy charting after an early-morning shift in the ER. Even though they were alone, she felt uncomfortable that he was so close, making the butterflies in her stomach flutter.

She cleared her throat and rubbed her neck, shifting away slightly. "Good morning, Captain."

"Formalities?"

"Yes." Her cheeks flamed with heat. "We are on duty, after all."

"Good point. My apologies, Commander. What happened while I was off duty?"

"There was a motor vehicle collision. Minor. One went to surgery with Lieutenant Drew." She handed the chart to Thorne.

"Why?" he asked, flipping through the pages.

"Spleen was bleeding too much. Lieutenant Drew is performing a splenectomy as we speak." She glanced at his watch. "Barring complications, he should be finished soon."

Thorne nodded. "Anything else?"

"Seven people with a cold, and a couple crewmen of the *Hope* stumbled in for help easing their hangovers before they boarded." She shook her head. "It was like a flash mob last night at Scooby's, a really inappropriate flash mob."

Thorne pulled out his phone and pulled up the web. "It was, in fact."

Erica leaned over to see the video from Scooby's, the choreographed movements to the song. "Pretty impressive for a bunch of drunkards."

"I know. Scooby was quite happy he got to film it." Thorne's eyes twinkled.

Erica laughed. "I bet he was. That man is obsessed with pop culture."

"Who?" Bunny asked, appearing behind the charge desk.

Erica jumped back from Thorne and cleared her throat again as she stared at the chart. "Sachiho."

Bunny cocked an eyebrow. "Who?"

"Scooby," Thorne interjected. "There was a bit of a scene of the weird kind last night at Scooby's bar."

Bunny chuckled. "When isn't there?"

"Is there something I can help you with, Bunny?" Erica asked, hoping that she could throw herself into busywork.

"Nope. I'm just about to head out. My shift is over." Bunny put the last of her charts away. "Have a good day, Commander and Captain."

Bunny left the two of them standing there at the charge desk alone.

"Why did that feel awkward?" Thorne asked.

"I have no idea."

Only she did. Well, at least she knew why she was feeling awkward, because she didn't want to be alone with Thorne again. Only, that was ridiculous. She was going to be alone with him again. Sex had changed it.

Your feelings for him, too.

"I thought you were going to watch some SEALs train

down at the aquatic center?" she asked, trying to sound nonchalant and failing.

"I might yet."

"What test is it?"

"Drown proofing. The next week there will be several rounds of it."

"Oh, that test looks brutal. I've seen it."

"It's hard-core. Though, I can't really demonstrate it anymore. I was pretty darn good at it, though." He smiled to himself.

"I'm sure you were. You swam in open water with an infected leg wound."

The smile disappeared. "Yes."

"I'm sorry. I didn't mean to bring it up. You don't like talking about it, do you?"

He shrugged. "I don't like to dwell on the past. I can't change it. Just got to keep one foot in front of the other and move forward; the future hasn't been written."

"So you don't believe things are predestined?"

He shook his head. "Nope and, if they were, I'd have to have some words with someone about the rough end of the stick I got a few times—and I'm not just talking about my leg."

Erica smiled. "I understand."

"Well, I better check on the lieutenant's surgery. Make sure the splenectomy is going smoothly and we don't lose the patient."

"I'll see you later."

"I hope so." He turned and left her standing there with her charts. She watched him walk away. There was just a slight limp to his gait, but he was still that strong, Navy SEAL Special Ops officer who had begged her not to take his leg.

There were so many admirable things about him. Also there were many annoying things about him. Maybe

Scooby was right. They were too volatile together. That was what Scooby had told Thorne and Thorne had told her.

What does Scooby know? He has green shag carpet on his ceilings and walls.

"I saw the way he looked at you and the way you looked at him."

Erica shook Regina's words from her head. They were the last words Regina had said to Erica before she'd walked back up the gang plank to board the *Hope.* Erica had had a break and had gone outside to watch as the *Hope* sailed east towards the States. She'd wished for a moment she was back on the ship headed for San Diego.

Not that she knew any one besides Regina and Rick in San Diego, but it was the gateway to a new port of call. Headquarters. It was one thing she'd loved about serving on the *Hope.* Every day was something new and exciting, but she'd only been able to go so far on the ship.

Here in Okinawa or another similar base she could rise above her current rank. That was, if she didn't mess it up by sleeping with her commanding officer.

Oh, wait: she had done that.

Erica pinched the bridge of her nose and shook her head. No, she couldn't let this escalate any further.

They'd shared one night of passion and that was all it could be.

Keep telling yourself that.

Her phone pinged with an email. She glanced down and saw it was from Admiral Greer. Confused as to why the admiral would be emailing, she opened it, reading it quickly. She almost dropped her phone and had to read the email again, her hands were shaking so bad.

All her hard work was about to pay off as her dream post was offered to her.

All she had to do now was tell Thorne she was leaving.

* * *

You're here to see SEAL training. That's it.

It was the end of the week of SEAL training and she was coming to watch that and not tell Thorne that she'd accepted a new posting at Annapolis in Maryland.

The email from Admiral Greer had been to promote her from commander to captain and offer her a position at the prestigious school. Her dream position. She'd said yes without a second thought. Now she had to tell Thorne and she was positive he'd understand.

At least that was what she kept trying to tell herself, but she wasn't a good liar. Even she didn't believe herself.

She'd always wanted to go and work at the United States Naval Academy. She'd be training medical corp recruits. It was something she'd always dreamed of, but the opportunity had never presented itself. After that fiasco in Rhode Island she'd never thought it would, to be honest.

Now it had, she had to jump at the chance. Even if it meant leaving Thorne behind.

He didn't make any promises. Neither did you.

This was her career. Love had screwed it up before and she couldn't let that happen again. No matter how much she wanted to stay with him.

The last time she'd chosen love over career it had burned her. Seriously burned her. And that hadn't even been love. That had just been lust.

With Thorne it was different. They connected.

And now she was leaving.

He'll understand.

If the situation was reversed, he would jump at the opportunity.

She snuck into the aquatic center and took a seat in the bleachers. The trainees were in the water doing their drown proofing, which consisted of bottom bouncing, floating and various retrievals. The test usually exhausted the swimmer, but also prepared them for rigorous missions.

Thorne was walking along the edge of the pool with another instructor. She could tell by the way he paced on the deck that he wanted to be in there with them, but couldn't.

He turned away from the testers and looked up at her. *Damn it.*

She wasn't ready for this. Blood rushed to her cheeks as he headed in her direction, up the few stairs to where she was sitting.

"Erica, what're you doing here?"

"I've never witnessed this particular test. I thought it might be interesting to watch."

He smiled and then sat down on the bench next to her. "You just came off an extremely long shift. I know because I scheduled it. You should be at home sleeping."

"I'm a bit tired, but I had to come see this." She looked closer. "I thought their hands are tied?"

"They will be; the instructor is just acclimatizing them, getting them ready for the test. These guys are pretty green. Besides, the instructor will pull them out of the water, freeze them out a bit."

"I bet they'll freeze."

"Get them used to hypothermia, but not really. This is a controlled environment and they won't be out of the water that long." And just as he said the words a whistle echoed and the trainees clambered out of the water as fast as they could. When they were standing to attention, that was when the instructors begin to tie the trainees' hands together.

"I thought my training at Annapolis was difficult," she muttered under her breath.

"You have to be tough to go on the kind of missions these men could go on."

"I don't doubt that. It's why I never even contemplated

becoming a SEAL. I just wanted to be in the Medical Corp. Going the officer route helped pay for that training."

"That's how I originally started," Thorne said a bit wistfully as he stared down at the group of ten seamen, dripping and trying not to shiver on the pool deck.

"What made you go into the SEALs?"

"The death of my twin brother." There was a sadness to his voice. One she was familiar with. One she had used herself when talking about her father. It was pain.

"I knew you had a brother, but I didn't know he was your twin. I'm sorry," she said and she placed a hand on his knee, at a loss for words. "How did you...? How did he...?"

"Die?" he asked.

"You don't have to tell me. I didn't mean to pry."

"It's okay."

Thorne ran his hand through his hair. "He died in service. He showed up at the field hospital I was stationed at. I was called off my ship to assist. In the field hospital there was an IED. There was an explosion and Liam died in my arms."

She took his hand in hers and squeezed it. "I'm sorry. So sorry."

"I appreciate the sentiment, but it was my fault."

"How?" she asked, confused.

"I don't want to get into it."

"I get it."

He glanced up at her. "Do you?"

"I do. I don't like talking about my father to many people."

Thorne nodded. "Did he die in service?"

Erica's stomach knotted. "No. He didn't."

She didn't talk about her father, not to anyone.

She sighed again. "He died as a result of service. He was wounded on a mission, came back home and the doctors cleared him—but I think the wound and losing most of his unit caused PTSD. He went back when he healed and was on a covert operation when he went AWOL, blowing the mission, and he was dishonorably discharged. It was then he killed himself."

"I'm sorry to hear that."

"He was my hero. If he could've got the help he needed..."

"I understand." He stared down at her hand, tracing the back with his thumb, which made her blood heat as she thought of his hands stroking her body.

"I better go." She took her hand back, feeling uncomfortable, and stood. She'd opened up to Thorne too much. It was dangerous letting him know that about her.

He opened up to you.

And that was a problem. She was scared.

"I'll walk you back to your quarters."

"It's broad daylight, Thorne. I think I can manage."

"I don't mind." The tone of his voice implied that he wouldn't take no for an answer. He was going to walk her back whether she liked it or not. She didn't mind it, except the fact that she might not be able to resist asking him inside.

Remember how Captain Seaton hurt you. Don't do this to yourself.

Only Thorne wasn't Captain Seaton. Thorne was different. He wouldn't report her as mentally unstable because she was taking a new position and leaving him.

At least that was what she kept trying to tell herself, but it was so hard to open up and trust again. She'd resigned herself a while ago to the fact that love was not to be a part of her life and then she'd met Thorne.

He limped slightly as they walked to her quarters.

"Why don't you go back?" Erica asked. "You don't have to do this. I am a big girl."

"It's not a bother. I needed to stretch my leg. The moisture actually bothers me sometimes. Phantom leg pain."

"I'm sorry you have to go through that."

"Most people do. With the trauma inflicted, the brain can't really understand why the nerves aren't there any longer. Besides, I was hoping you can give me another massage sometime."

She laughed. "Oh, really? So that was your master plan—take me home and, instead of letting me sleep, I'm supposed to massage you?"

"Well, we could do something else."

Heat bloomed in her cheeks. "Thorne, I don't think it's wise. Do you?"

Then he pulled her close to him. "No, it's not wise, but I can't resist you. Believe me, I've tried. I want to resist you."

Her pulse thundered in her ears. She was pressed against his chest and very aware of how close they were.

"Thorne," she whispered, closing her eyes so she wouldn't be drawn into his eyes, which always seemed to melt her. "I can't. I just…I can't."

"Why?"

"I thought we were going to be friends?"

Thorne let go of her. "I'm sorry, Erica. I wanted to respect your wishes. I did, but when I'm around you I can't help myself. I didn't… I don't want a relationship. I can't give you a relationship."

"And I can't give you one either." She reached up and touched his cheek. "I can't be with another commanding officer. The last time I got involved with someone I work for it almost cost me my career. Unless you can promise me a lifetime, unless you can promise me that our relationship won't affect my career, then I just can't. I can't."

Because I'm leaving.

Only she couldn't verbalize those words.

Chicken.

She tried to turn and leave, because she was embarrassed she'd admitted it to him. Embarrassed that he knew she'd been foolish enough once to believe in forever with someone who wasn't worthy. She made it to her quarters and opened the door. Just as Thorne came up behind her.

"Erica, I would never jeopardize your career. I hope you know that."

"I know. I just wanted you to know why... I couldn't really hide it any longer. I thought for sure you knew. I was pretty sure it was on my service record."

"No, why would it be? If you were passed up for commendation or a promotion in rank, do you really think those responsible for denying that would record it on your service record?"

She was a bit stunned.

"You look surprised," he commented.

"Captain Dayton knew why I was passed up for promotion. I don't even know why he actually picked me to come aboard the *Hope.*"

"Captain Dayton is a smart man. He saw talent. Just like I did." Thorne rubbed the back of his neck, frowning, as if he was struggling to tell her something and she was expecting him to tell her why he couldn't be with someone.

What was holding him back?

What's holding you back?

Still she waited. She waited for him to open up to her, waited pathetically for a sign that maybe it would be worth a second thought. Only he said nothing to her and she was angry at herself for even thinking for one moment that she'd give up on her dreams for a man. When had she become so weak?

Her career mattered. Her life mattered.

"Thorne, I have something to tell you."

"Erica, don't say something we'll regret."

"I'm transferring to Annapolis."

The blood drained from his face and his brow furrowed. "Pardon?"

"I'm transferring to Annapolis, Maryland. I was offered a position as Captain and I would be working with medical corps recruits. It's a chance of a lifetime and I couldn't turn it down."

"No, of course not." He smiled, but it was forced. "Who gave you the commendation?"

"Captain Dayton actually recommended me."

He chuckled, but it was one of derision, not mirth. "Is that a fact? When do you leave?"

"In a week."

Thorne nodded slowly. "Well, of course you have to go."

"I do." Only part of her was screaming not to go—the part of her that wanted to stay with Thorne, marry him and settle down. But he couldn't give her any promises and neither could she. If he didn't want her, she didn't want to settle down with a man who would resent her down the road or, worse, she would resent him for making her give up on her career.

No, she had to go.

"I'm sorry I'm leaving you without a second in command."

"I'll make do until a replacement can be sent." He wasn't looking at her as he backed away from her door. "I better put in a request now."

"Do you still need me to look at your leg?"

"No," he snapped. "It's fine. I'll see you tomorrow, Commander Griffin."

Her heart ached as she watched him walk away quickly and she tried to tell herself it was all for the best.

This way she wouldn't get hurt.

* * *

It was her last day. She was shipping out tonight, but this was her last day working at the base hospital. Her last day working with Thorne.

Things had been awkward since she'd told him that she was accepting a post in Annapolis. They spoke, but barely, and it was about work. She waited for the other shoe to drop. She waited for him to report her as unfit or something.

And when the conversation drifted from work or the duty roster it became tense. It was like he was mad that she was leaving. But it was part of life in the Navy. Officers took postings, left postings.

Her promotion to captain was something she couldn't give up but, anytime she went to talk to him about it, he turned and walked away from her, making it blatantly obvious that he was avoiding her.

She'd even gone to Scooby's a few times, trying to catch him. Only he hadn't been there and Scooby was even concerned he hadn't seen Thorne in a while.

"He shouldn't be alone, Commander. He thinks he can handle it. He can't. I know he's not the only one around here."

Erica was sure that last part was a jab at her. Scooby didn't understand her circumstances. He didn't get why she couldn't be with someone again. She couldn't tether herself to another person and Annapolis was the dream.

It had been since she'd graduated there.

Only, being around Thorne had made her think for a moment that maybe it might be good to be with someone. She wanted it to be him, but he didn't seem to have an interest in letting her past his barriers.

"Commander!" Bunny shouted from the charge desk, a phone in her hand. "Commander Griffin."

Erica rushed over. "What's wrong?"

"It's a code black," Bunny whispered. "You're to go out to the helipad. The west part of the trauma floor is being cleared. Need to know only."

"Tell them I'm on my way." Erica started running toward the helipad. The wing in question was being cleared quickly and Masters of Arms were beginning to block off the entrances and barricade people from that section of the trauma floor.

A shudder traveled down her spine as she thought of that moment five years ago: silent running on the ship. Pitch-black, and the flare from the submarine illuminating the sky to direct the helicopter.

Another covert operation.

When she got to the helipad Thorne was there waiting, the helipad surrounded by armed military police.

"It's about time," Thorne snapped.

"Who's coming in? The president or something?"

"They didn't say. Just that it was covert. Most likely Special Ops."

The roar of the helicopter sounded in the distance and they braced themselves for the wind being stirred up as the helicopter landed. Once they had the all clear they ran forward with the gurney and loaded the patient, who was screaming in agony.

The patient's commanding officer leaped down beside the gurney and helped them wheel the man toward the hospital.

"Prepare for more incoming," the commanding officer said. "We had a few casualties, but he was by far the worst."

"Do we get any specifics?" Erica snapped. "Or do we refer to him as John Doe?"

"Commander Griffin!" Thorne warned.

"John Doe, Commander," the unit's commanding officer responded. "It's all classified."

"Understood," Thorne said. "We'll take care of your man. What happened to him?"

"Explosion. Shredded his arm. We packed it the best we could, but I think it's infected."

"Are you medical?" Erica asked sharply as they wheeled the John Doe into a triage room and began to undress him to get to the damage.

"I am."

"Maybe you can scrub in," Thorne suggested.

"I can't. As soon as the men are stable we have to ship to our meeting place."

Erica snorted and Thorne sent her a look to silence her.

The moment Erica came close to the man's left arm, he screamed in pain, and as soon as she got close to him she could see the infection. It was worse than Thorne's had been. She didn't know how long these men had been in the field, but this John Doe was lucky to be alive.

"He needs surgery," Erica said, turning quickly to start a central line to get antibiotics into the John Doe and sedate him.

"Agreed," Thorne said. "Don't worry, seaman, we'll take care of you."

Erica had the central line in as fast as she could and was pumping the medicine the John Doe needed. He was also severely dehydrated, by the way his lips were cracked, and she couldn't help but wonder how much blood loss he was suffering from.

Thorne sedated him and then was inserting tubes down the man's throat so that he could breathe.

After a few orders, the nurses who were in the know had the OR ready to go and they were wheeling their John Doe off to surgery.

Erica scrubbed alongside Thorne as the nurses prepped and draped the patient.

"Pretty basic, I think," she said.

"What's basic?" Thorne asked.

"Amputation of the arm."

Thorne stopped scrubbing for a moment. "If it's deemed necessary."

"I think it's necessary. Don't you?"

Thorne ignored her and walked into the OR where a nurse gowned him and put gloves on him.

Erica cursed under her breath and followed him, jamming her arms angrily down into the gown that was held out for her.

As she approached the table she could see the damage the IED had caused and this time she did curse out loud.

Thorne glanced at her quickly. "I know."

"He's lucky to have lived this long. Do you think it can still be saved, Captain?" The tone was sarcastic. It was meant to be, but then the scrub nurse beside Thorne gasped, and few others looked at her like she'd lost her mind.

She was being insubordinate to her commanding officer in his OR.

"Get out," Thorne said.

"What?" Erica asked.

"I said, get out."

"Why? He obviously needs an amputation. Are you telling me that you're going to work on his arm when it's clearly not salvageable?"

"That will be my decision as head surgeon. Now, Commander Griffin, if you'd kindly leave my OR and send in Ensign Benjamin. He's been cleared for this level of security and he can assist me in saving John Doe's life."

"With all due respect, Captain. I'm scrubbed in and ready to go. I've dealt with infections of this caliber before. I think I should be the one assisting."

"Do you?"

"I do." Erica held her ground. She had nothing to lose anyway, as she was heading to Annapolis.

"I don't think so, Commander. You wrote off his arm before you had X-rays done or even thoroughly examined the wound. Is that how you made your decision when you took my leg and ruined my career?"

The room was silent—at least, she assumed it was, since her head was filled with the thundering of her blood as it boiled.

She thought he'd forgiven her or didn't blame her for the decision she'd made five years ago, which had taken his leg, but apparently that wasn't true. He still resented her. Enough to bring up her competence in front of other staff members; he'd humiliated and embarrassed her.

Erica took a calming breath and stared at him across the OR.

"I saved your life."

"And I will save his. Now, get out of my OR, Commander. That's an order."

Erica didn't say anything but obeyed her commanding officer. She ripped off the gloves and gown and jammed them in the soiled bin and then scrubbed out as quickly as she could. When she was in the hall, she ripped off her surgical cap and tossed it against the wall.

She'd been so foolish to fall in love with her commanding officer, a former patient, even. She was stupid to think about trying to make it work, to think of having it all and settling down. She was weak for letting herself be momentarily ruled by her heart.

Well, it wouldn't happen again. She would never open her heart again.

She was tired of it being broken.

Thorne couldn't save the John Doe's arm. Erica had been right. He'd known from the moment he'd seen it briefly in the triage room, but instead of listening to her he'd been ruled by his emotions, by the feelings of betrayal he'd felt ever since she'd told him that she was leaving Okinawa to take a prestigious posting at Annapolis.

If it had been anyone else he would've been happier for them. He was happy for Erica, but the fact was she was leaving him, and he was acting like a fool.

She was leaving and he didn't want to let her go.

This is what you wanted, wasn't it?

He deserved this. He didn't deserve to be happy. It was fitting she was leaving.

He wanted her to leave Okinawa so he wouldn't be tempted, the only problem being he'd been tempted long before she'd decided to leave and now he didn't want her to go. He wanted her to stay with him. Only, she couldn't.

Thorne had to let her go.

It was for the best.

She would move on.

Erica wanted to advance her career: it was evident from the postings she'd chosen, by how far she'd come and what she'd endured to get to her position.

He couldn't be selfish, because he couldn't promise her anything.

Why not?

So he had to let her go. But first it was up to him to explain to the John Doe how his career was over and up to him to see the Special Ops team off to wherever they were going. Most likely San Diego.

As he headed out into the private room where the team was waiting, he caught sight of Erica in her uniform, her rucksack over her bag. She'd obviously cleared out her locker.

Let her go. She's mad at you and doesn't want to speak with you.

"Commander Griffin."

She turned and faced him. Her expression was unreadable as she dropped her bag and saluted him, holding herself at attention.

"Erica," he said.

"Captain." She would not look him in the eye.

"You're being ridiculous."

Her eyes narrowed and she looked at him, but wouldn't speak to him.

"You're at ease, Commander."

Erica relaxed her posture. "Can I help you, Captain?"

"I need to speak with you. Privately."

"I don't think that's wise, Captain. I think everything has been said."

"Please."

Erica sighed and picked up her rucksack, following Thorne into a small exam room. She shut the door behind her.

"What do you need to talk to me about? Whatever it is, make it quick. I'm catching the next transport back to the US."

"I know. I wanted to apologize."

"Apologize."

"I was out of line. You're right; the John Doe lost his arm. There was no way to salvage it."

Erica frowned. "I'm sorry that it couldn't be saved. I am."

Thorne nodded and then reached into his lab coat pocket for the small package he'd been carrying around since before she'd been leaving. Maybe because on some certain level he always knew she'd leave. "There was no excuse for my behavior. I wanted to clear the air before you left and give you this."

Erica glanced at the box with trepidation. "What is it?"

"Open it."

She shook her head and handed it back to him. "I can't accept this."

"You can. It's just a token, a reminder of your month here in Okinawa Prefecture."

Erica opened the box and pulled out the tiny bottle full of sand. "Sand?"

"It's from Iriomote Island, a bit of a distance from here, but it's *hoshizuna*—also known as star sand."

A brief smile passed on her face. "Thank you."

"Good luck."

She paused and then nodded. "Thank you, Captain."

Say something.

Only Thorne couldn't express what he wanted to say to her. He couldn't tell her how he felt; he just stood there frozen, numb, as she picked up her rucksack and turned to open the door. He moved quickly and held his hand against the door.

"Thorne, what're you doing?" she demanded. "I'll miss my transport."

"Stay," he said. "I'm sorry for kicking you out of my OR. That won't happen again. Just stay."

"Why should I?" she asked.

"You're my second in command. The best I've had since I took this posting."

"That's the only reason? Because I'm a good commander?"

No. That's not the only reason.

"Yes."

She shook her head. "I can't stay, Thorne. I'm being promoted to captain and to a position I've dreamed about holding for a long time. I'm sorry, but I have to go."

"What more do you want from me?" he snapped. "I can't give you any more than that. If you were expecting something more after our night together, I made it very clear."

"As did I," she said. "I should've known better than get involved with a commanding officer again."

"I'm not that man."

"You basically questioned my judgment in that OR."

"I apologized for that!" Thorne shouted. "What more do you want from me, Erica?"

"Nothing. There's nothing I want or need from you. Let me go, and please don't damage my professional reputation."

He clenched his fists. "Do you think I would damage your career out of spite?"

"You're not the first. It took me a long time to earn back what shred of respect I have and now I'm finally getting the promotion I deserve. I won't let anyone take that away from me."

"You obviously don't know me."

"I thought I did."

"You don't because you must think so little of me to think that I would stoop to Captain Seaton's level."

The blood drained from her face. "I never mentioned his name before."

"The name of your former commanding officer is on your record and, since I know you didn't have an affair with Dayton, I put two and two together. You really get around with your commanding officers, don't you?"

The sting of her slap rocked him. He deserved it. What he'd said was out of line and totally inappropriate.

"Goodbye, Captain Wilder."

And this time he didn't stop her from leaving.

He'd severed the tie and let her go.

CHAPTER FOURTEEN

It was best to let her go.

Was it?

No, it wasn't. Erica had been gone a week and he missed her. The guilt ate at him for the things he'd said to her. It made him angry when he thought about it. If Liam had heard him speak that way he would've beat his butt. Day to day he just moved through the motions; sometimes he wasn't aware of the passing of the day. Another mistake he'd made, and he had to live with it, but it was difficult.

Things she'd brought alive were dull and gray in comparison now. He went to Scooby's every night and all he could hear was her laughter above the noise. When he glanced at the green shag carpet in the Jungle Room, and saw the booth they'd shared, his stomach would knot up.

And the pineapple pizza… He couldn't stomach it.

"You miss her."

Scooby had said that numerous times, but Thorne had never deigned to respond to him. He was trying to ignore the obvious, because if he ignored it, if he pretended it hadn't happened, then it wouldn't hurt so much.

The pain would go away.

Yeah, right.

Her quarters were still empty, waiting on the next commanding officer to take over. He walked by them daily, thinking about how she'd opened up to him about why she couldn't be in a relationship and he'd said nothing at all.

Just kept her out, because he'd thought it would be for the best.

A quick break.

Only, no matter how he tried to purge her from his system, he couldn't. She'd haunted him for five years before she'd come to the base. Now that he knew her, now that he'd touched, kissed and caressed the woman of his fantasies, he couldn't expel her to the dark corners of his mind.

She wasn't just a memory to look back on fondly. She was everywhere, even in his flesh. There was no way he could purge her from his system and he didn't want to.

Erica was so much more and he was too obtuse to see that.

"You look deep in thought," Scooby remarked, setting down a beer.

"What?" Thorne glanced around and didn't even realize that his walk had led him to Scooby's place or that he'd sat down at the bar. He rubbed his face and groaned.

"I said you look deep in thought, but not anymore. Sorry for interrupting your thoughts, Captain, but you looked a bit like a zombie."

"As long as I wasn't moaning." Thorne took a quick swig of beer, but it was flat in his mouth.

"How can I help you, Captain? I hate seeing you walking around here like some *deretto* fool."

"Deretto?"

"Love-struck."

Thorne snorted. "Who said I was love-struck?"

"The expression on your face speaks volumes. I may be old, Captain Wilder, but I'm not blind. You were in love with her."

"No. I'm not." Only he was, but he didn't deserve her. Because someone who was in love with someone didn't hurt them the way he'd hurt her. They didn't deserve to have a happy ending. He didn't deserve love.

"You're pulling my leg, Captain. You love Commander Griffin and she loves you."

Thorne chuckled. "She doesn't love me. Well, she may have, but not anymore. Not after the way I hurt her."

"Hurt her? What did you do to her?"

"I said some things I regret and she left." He touched the side of his face where she'd slapped him a week ago. It still hurt.

After he'd talked to the Navy SEALs about the John Doe, he'd gone out to arrange their transport and had seen Erica heading across the tarmac. Without thinking, he'd run after her, calling her name. She'd turned and looked, but ignored him as she boarded the plane.

He deserved it.

He didn't deserve her.

"You said things to her? What kind of things?"

"It doesn't matter. She's gone."

Scooby reached across the bar and gave him a quick smack upside the head. *"Baka!"*

"What? Why did you do that?"

"Idiot. You're an idiot, Captain Wilder." Scooby shook his head and uttered a few more choice swear words in Japanese. Probably all of which meant Thorne was an idiot or worse.

"What the heck have I done to you lately, Scooby?"

"Fuzakeru na! Stop being stupid, Captain Wilder. Go after her."

"Who?"

That earned him another cuff around the head and another oath in his direction. "Commander Griffin. You need to go to Minneapolis and get her back."

"You mean Annapolis."

"Isn't it the same?"

"No."

Scooby shrugged. "I've heard of Minneapolis. I've been to Minneapolis. Where is Annapolis?"

"Maryland."

"And that's not near Minneapolis?"

Thorne shook his head. "No."

"Then you need to go there. Tell her how you feel and apologize for your obtuseness. Apologize for driving her away, like you've always driven away people who try to become close to you."

"It's not that simple."

"*Fuzakeru na!* Of course it's simple. You love her, don't you?"

Yes. Still, he couldn't say it out loud.

He'd been hiding it from himself for so long, trying to suppress it, but, yes, he loved her. He was in love with Erica and he was an idiot for letting her go.

For so long he'd fought love, but maybe it was worth the risk. It was better than living a numbed existence. Still, he didn't deserve it. Not after what he'd done to Liam.

Liam never blamed you. Liam would want you to be happy. Stop blaming yourself.

But it was hard to let go of years of blame.

Tyler.

It went off like a lightbulb. Tyler had come to him a couple of years ago to apologize for his mistake which had cost Thorne his leg.

It had torn Tyler up inside to know he was responsible.

Thorne had sat him down and told Tyler that it wasn't his fault and that he didn't blame Tyler for the loss of his leg. It was part of serving. Thorne had told Tyler to let go of his guilt and get on with his life.

Yet, he hadn't done that.

He was a hypocrite.

The John Doe had been disappointed that he'd lost an

arm and could no longer serve, but he'd put a positive spin on it.

"At least my wife will be glad that I'll be home permanently."

Even the John Doe had someone waiting for him. Liam had had a wife and two beautiful kids. Neither of them had been afraid of serving their country and coming home to their families. Why was he so scared?

"I can't just leave my command. I have to arrange for a leave."

"Bah, you're making excuses."

"I'm not making excuses." He closed his eyes. "Maybe I am, Scooby. I don't know why I'm so…"

"Afraid?" Scooby shook his head. "Love, it sucks. It's hard and painful, but it's worth it."

"I've always said you're a man of many layers, Scooby."

He nodded. "Well, when you own a bar where a lot of different armed forces personnel move through, you pick up the odd thing. You all think the same thing: you're not afraid to lay down your life for your country, but when it comes to matters of the heart a lot of you are a bit more hesitant. Love is a powerful thing."

"Is it only the men?" Thorne asked.

"No, it's not. Commander Griffin is scared. I know she is. You two are the same and I believe I told you that when she first arrived here. You two are so volatile."

"I don't think you quite know what volatile means."

Scooby cursed under his breath. "Bah, you know what I mean. You two are both hotheaded, stubborn officers. You'll rub each other the wrong way, but you're meant to be together. Nobody else can put up with you."

"I'll arrange for a replacement and a transport."

"Good! You do that, Captain. Make the arrangements and go."

"And if she still doesn't want me?"

Scooby shrugged. "Then it's her loss, but at least you'll have closure."

"Thanks, Scooby. I think." Thorne set money down on the counter. "Though, you do know 'volatile' means something explosive?"

"Exactly my point, Captain. Now, get out of here."

Thorne chuckled. "Thanks."

"No problem." Scooby moved down the bar, muttering under his breath.

Even though he didn't deserve Erica, even though he'd messed it all up, he was going to try. He was brave enough to find out the answer—and if it was yes. If she loved him, he'd make it up to her even if it took him the rest of his life.

One month later, Annapolis, Maryland.

Erica had been paged by the recruitment office, something about a new plebe for the medical corps that they were eager to have at Annapolis.

She wasn't sure why they needed her there, but since it came from Admiral Greer she wasn't going to question anything, even though she was just about to head into class. Thankfully her second in command could take over the class while she dealt with this special request.

As she moved across the grounds, the trees were just starting to bloom with the first sign of spring and the red tulips in the center green were waving slightly in the warm breeze. It was familiar and, even though she was by the sea, she kind of missed being in Japan.

She absolutely loved her new position at Annapolis, but often there were times her mind drifted back to Okinawa.

There'd been a difference in the air there and it had been nice to see palm trees and white beaches. Not that Maryland wasn't beautiful, with the colonial charm and tall sails filling Chesapeake Bay; it was the company she missed.

Thorne.

She missed him and she didn't realize how much. Her day-to-day operations at Annapolis were just an existence.

Maybe it was because she was now a teacher at the most prestigious academy in the United States, but there was none of the familiarity or comraderie that she'd had when she'd been in Okinawa or serving on board the *Hope.*

Her commanding officer wasn't close to her age. He was older and didn't seem to have much of a sense of humor. Admiral Greer seemed to live on pomp, circumstance and regulations. So when she wasn't doing a shift at the base hospital where she could be in scrubs, the rest of the time she had to stay in her everyday dress uniform and heels.

She hated heels.

So, yeah, there was a lot to miss about Okinawa, but for the most part it was Thorne. When she'd left Ginowan she didn't realize how lonely she was until her companionship was gone.

It tore her heart out to leave him, but it was obvious that he didn't feel the same way as she did. Not after that fiasco in the OR when he'd made it quite clear that he still blamed her for the loss of his leg. When he'd thrown her out of his ER she'd tried to get him out of her mind—then he'd apologized and for a brief moment she'd thought he was going to open up to her. Instead he'd hurt her.

He'd expected her to give up on her dream so that she could stay with him. That was something she couldn't do.

Even though she was in love with him. Because there was no point in denying it: she loved Thorne. But she couldn't give up the life she'd mapped out for herself. Just like she didn't expect him to give up his life and his command posting in Okinawa.

It was cruel how love worked out that way sometimes. They were not meant to be together and she had to try and forget him.

Which was not easy.

She'd tried to do just that, but to no avail because, instead of the mysterious stranger with the intense blue eyes who had called her an angel, the Thorne she'd fallen for invaded her dreams. Every time she closed her eyes he was there.

So real and intense. She could recall his kisses, his touch. He was everywhere, his memory haunting her like a ghost. In the naval base hospital when she saw wounded warriors coming through, trying to heal themselves and continue to serve, she saw Thorne's determination to continue on.

Or, when watching a batch of plebes training to become Navy SEALs by drown proofing in the pool, all she had to do was close her eyes and picture him watching them, his arms crossed, assessing them.

Or when she went out and had a slice of pineapple pizza, which didn't hold a candle to Scooby's house specialty.

It pained her physically not be with him.

She'd grown numb.

Don't let him in now.

Right now she had a job to do. There was no room for Thorne in her mind. She didn't know why she was thinking of him constantly.

You miss him.

Erica took a deep breath and stopped to glance up at the blue spring sky. Yeah, she did miss him.

When she had started to unpack she'd found the star-shaped bottle with the sand. The one he'd given to her.

She'd almost thrown it out, trying to sever the tie, but she couldn't bring herself to do it. Because, even though he'd made it clear he didn't want her and didn't care for her, she loved him. She wished things between them had been different, but it was the way it was.

Besides, he didn't want her. He'd let her go.

He'd severed the ties long before she'd left Okinawa.

With a deep breath to ground herself, she headed up the white steps of the building she'd been asked to report to.

Before she headed into the recruitment office, she tidied her hair in a mirror and straightened her dress uniform jacket.

"Captain Griffin, the new recruit is waiting in room 407," Lieutenant Knox said, rising from his seat from behind his desk. He handed her the file.

"Thank you, Lieutenant." She flipped open the file. "A Navy SEAL?"

"Yes, Captain."

"His name is John Doe?" Erica asked, annoyed.

"Yes. I wasn't given specifics about why he stated his name was John Doe. He was quite unbending."

"He has to have a name. Why wouldn't he give you specifics?"

Lieutenant Knox shrugged. "Perhaps he's Special Ops. I don't know. I didn't see him. He was ushered in under a covert detail."

Erica was confused. "A covert detail? This doesn't make any sense."

"I'm sorry, Captain. That's all the intel I have."

Erica nodded and then headed to room 407. She didn't know what was going on here, but she was tired of covert operations and Navy SEALs. She'd taken this position at Annapolis to escape all that. There was only so much she could take in one lifetime of Special Ops, Navy SEALs and secrecy.

And she was tired of reminders of Thorne.

She knocked once and headed into the room. "Seaman, I understand you want to join the Med…"

She gasped and almost dropped the file in her hands, because they were shaking so bad. Standing in front of her in his dress whites was Thorne. He took off his white cap quickly and tucked it under his arm.

"Captain Griffin." He saluted her.

"C-Captain Wilder?"

He smiled. "Yes."

"What're you doing here? You're already a member of the Medical Corp."

"I know."

"Then why are you at the recruitment office?"

"I called in a favor from the admiral." Thorne set his cap down on the desk and took a step toward her.

"What kind of favor?" Her pulse began to race; he looked so good in his dress uniform. She'd never seen him in it. It suited him and made her weak in the knees.

Jerk. Remember what he did to you. How much it hurt.

"I told the admiral that I made a foolish error letting my second in command come to Annapolis."

"This is about getting me transferred back to Okinawa?" Rage boiled inside her. She threw the file at him, which he dodged. "Get out!"

"That's not why I'm here."

Only she wasn't going to listen to him. "How dare you? I'm not going to return to Okinawa as your commander. I can't believe you traveled halfway around the world to start up this old fight. You…you…."

"Erica, would you just calm down a minute and listen to me?" He tried to pull her to him, but she brushed off his embrace.

"Don't touch me—and it's Captain Griffin!"

"Erica," he said sternly. "I'm not here to take you back to Okinawa."

"You're not?"

"No, I'm not. Besides, that's not my posting any longer."

"What?" she asked in disbelief.

"I took an open position here at Annapolis."

"You what?" She took a step back and then leaned against the wall to collect herself. "You transferred here, but why?"

He smiled at her, those blue eyes twinkling. "Isn't it obvious?"

"No. It's not." Her voice shook as she braced herself. It was obvious, but she was in disbelief about it.

"I love you."

Erica's knees wobbled as the words sank in. "You love me?"

Thorne nodded. "I tried to resist you. I tried to wipe you from my mind, I tried not let you in. I told myself after my brother died in my arms and I saw the pain on his widow's face, the hole left in his children's hearts, that I wouldn't ever allow someone to mourn me. I joined the SEALs to fulfill my brother's dream and I blamed myself for Liam's death, and for that I felt I didn't deserve any kind of happiness."

"I don't understand what you're trying to tell me."

He ran his hands through his hair. "I was happy as a SEAL and then on a covert operation I was injured saving another man's life and I met you. You entranced me. My foggy memories had one bright spot and it was you. Of course, then I actually did meet you, and you weren't exactly as angelic as I thought you were in my fantasies."

Erica chuckled at that. "I'm not gentle. Must be the Cajun in me."

"I'm sorry for trying to shut you out, for embarrassing

you that day when the John Doe came in. You were right. He lost his arm. It was too far gone and, what I said? I was out of line."

Erica nodded. "I know. I saw his medical chart when he returned to San Diego. You did a good job with his amputation. As for the other things, well, I wasn't exactly easy on you."

"Thank you." Thorne closed the distance between them again. "Look, I just couldn't tell you how I felt about you, because I didn't think I deserved it. How could I be happy when I'm the reason Liam lost his life?"

"You deserve to be happy."

Thorne took a step closer. "So do you."

"Perhaps."

"I don't know what the future holds for me or you, but I know one thing: I love you and I can't live without you. It's worth the risk to be with you. I need to be with you, Erica."

She couldn't believe he was saying the words that she herself hadn't known she was longing to hear, but now that he was saying them she knew that she could have both her career and him. Something she never thought before. Most men had been intimidated by her rank, her career, except Thorne.

He was her match in every way.

Thorne ran his knuckles down her cheek. "I love you, Erica. I'm sorry for being such a…"

She suggested a word in Cajun and laughed at her secret joke.

"Sure, but I'm not sure I should admit to anything you say in Cajun."

"Then how about 'I forgive you'?"

Thorne smiled. "That I can live with."

He leaned forward and kissed her. His lips were gentle, urging, and she melted in his arms, totally forgetting that she was angry at him, that he'd hurt her, because he was sorry for what he'd done. He hadn't meant it. Thorne had tried to push her away just as much as she'd tried to push him away, but as Scooby had said they were "volatile" together.

Explosive. And, even though they were a combustible match, they were made for each other. They both had just been too stubborn to see it.

"What're you smiling about?" he asked.

"Something my *mamère* said."

"You better keep it to yourself."

"Why?" she asked.

"I don't want to be left in the dark with all the Cajun words."

Erica kissed him. "I promise to fill you in on Cajun when I can, but then again maybe not, as I have an advantage over you when you tick me off."

Thorne rolled his eyes, but laughed. "Well, I have to get used to living stateside again."

"Are you sorry you left Okinawa?" she asked.

"I'll miss it, I won't lie, but you're more important to me. I can get used to having soft-shell crab instead of pineapple pizza."

"Have you ever had soft-shell crab?"

"No."

She grinned. "Well, I hope you'll let me take you for your first time."

"Deal."

"I'm sorry too, for what it's worth."

"For what?" he asked.

"For walking away. For being insubordinate to my commanding officer on numerous occasions and for not telling you that I love you too."

He grinned. "Well, there are ways you can make it up to me."

"Is that so? Well, I can start off by giving you a massage."

"Oh, yes." He cupped her face and stroked her cheek. "That's a good start But first I have to check in officially."

"I'll take you there."

Hand in hand, they walked out of the recruitment office.

EPILOGUE

One year later, Annapolis, Maryland.

ERICA'S HEART RACED and she was shaking as she stood in a small anteroom off the side of the chapel on the naval base, a historic building. She thought if she was ever going to take the plunge and get married she was going to have her ceremony at the Naval Academy Chapel.

There were so many things architecturally about this chapel she loved. So much represented her core beliefs about being in the Navy. Like the stained glass window of Sir Galahad and his ideals which every Naval officer tried to live up to; and the domed ceiling, which reminded her of a cathedral in Florence, Italy, and was beautiful to look at.

Of course, when she'd originally had that thought when she was going for training here, she hadn't thought it would actually come to pass because she hadn't thought that she'd actually get married.

It hadn't mattered if she ever got married, until she'd met Thorne. Even if he'd never asked her, she'd have been happy with the life they were living in Annapolis. Both of them had been furthering their careers in the Navy, saving lives and training recruits when the proposal had happened. She hadn't been expecting it. They'd been walking along the shore a month ago, watching the sailboats with the colorful sails moving across the blue water, when he'd cried out in pain, dropping to his knee.

When she'd tried to see if he was okay, worried it was his phantom leg pain, he'd opened a small velvet box and proposed.

It was like something out of a dream; she still felt a bit dazed by it all.

And now she was standing in the antechamber, her knees knocking under the white silk of a very simple wedding dress.

"You could've worn your Navy uniform," Commander Rick Kettle, Regina's husband, whispered in her ear. "You are a captain."

"No, she's not!" Regina screeched and Erica chuckled.

"She's a captain, Regina. She has every right to wear her dress uniform."

Regina shot her husband the stink eye. "She looks beautiful and she's going to get married like a proper bride. This is a momentous occasion."

Rick shook his head and Erica glared at Regina, who was rocking back and forth, holding her newborn daughter named after Erica.

"If you weren't holding my goddaughter you would be in serious trouble, my friend."

Regina winked. "Well, at least it got your mind off your nerves, now, didn't it?"

Erica was going to say more when there was a knock at the door and Erica's mother stuck her head into the room. Erica had resolved things with her mother and, even though her mother didn't totally agree with Erica's career choice, she'd absolutely been won over by Thorne. The rift between her and her mom was healing and she was very excited to be a part of the wedding.

"It's time."

Regina came over and squeezed Erica's arm. "You can do this!"

Erica nodded, but she was still shaking.

Regina and her mother left the anteroom. Erica didn't have any bridesmaids because the only man Thorne had wanted to stand up with him was his brother and he couldn't have that. So they'd both opted to keep the wedding small.

The only people attending were close friends and family.

Erica would've liked Captain Dayton to walk her down the aisle, but he was out at sea on the *Hope,* so Regina's husband was stepping in, and he did look quite dashing in his white dress uniform.

"You ready to go?"

"Yes; if I linger too much longer I might bolt from sheer terror."

"As long as it's not Captain Wilder making you bolt."

"No," Erica said and then smiled. "No, not him."

Rick smiled and took her arm. "Left and then right, Captain Griffin. Just one foot in front of the other."

Erica nodded and he walked her out of the antechamber to the main chapel. The large pipe organ began to play the bridal song, but she couldn't hear it over the sound of her pulse thundering in her ears.

As she started walking up the aisle there was a call out and a salute, which caused her to gasp, as a group of Navy SEALs decked out in their dress uniforms stood at attention for her, their sabers hanging at their sides.

They were Thorne's old unit. She recognized Mick the commanding officer she'd stood up to all those years ago on the *Hope*—and then she got a glimpse of Thorne standing there in his dress uniform and suddenly she wasn't so nervous any longer.

She walked up the aisle and glanced at all their friends

and family; she welled up when she saw Bunny and Scooby in the aisle, smiling at her. Scooby bowed quickly, beaming at her. She stopped Rick, breaking rank, so she could hug them briefly, trying not to cry.

When she got to the front Thorne took her hand. She didn't even remember the ceremony, because all she could see was Thorne—the man who'd had no name when she'd first met him but was full of fight, spirit and a passion to serve his country.

He enchanted her and enraged her at times. They were volatile together, so explosive, and Erica loved every minute of it.

Before she knew it, she was kissing her husband to an audience that was cheering and clapping.

"Are you okay?" Thorne whispered in her ear.

"I'm fine, why?"

"You look a bit shocked."

"A deer trapped in barbed wire?"

Thorne chuckled. "Headlights. I'm buying a book of old sayings for our first anniversary."

Erica pinched him as they headed down the aisle. "If we survive that long."

"We will."

"How do you know?" she teased. They paused at the entrance of the chapel as his old unit raised their sabers in a salute. Erica and Thorne passed under them, kissing at the end.

"Because I love you and I'm never letting you go."

* * * * *

MILLS & BOON®
Hardback – July 2015

ROMANCE

MILLS & BOON®
Large Print – July 2015

ROMANCE

The Taming of Xander Sterne	Carole Mortimer
In the Brazilian's Debt	Susan Stephens
At the Count's Bidding	Caitlin Crews
The Sheikh's Sinful Seduction	Dani Collins
The Real Romero	Cathy Williams
His Defiant Desert Queen	Jane Porter
Prince Nadir's Secret Heir	Michelle Conder
The Renegade Billionaire	Rebecca Winters
The Playboy of Rome	Jennifer Faye
Reunited with Her Italian Ex	Lucy Gordon
Her Knight in the Outback	Nikki Logan

HISTORICAL

The Soldier's Dark Secret	Marguerite Kaye
Reunited with the Major	Anne Herries
The Rake to Rescue Her	Julia Justiss
Lord Gawain's Forbidden Mistress	Carol Townend
A Debt Paid in Marriage	Georgie Lee

MEDICAL

How to Find a Man in Five Dates	Tina Beckett
Breaking Her No-Dating Rule	Amalie Berlin
It Happened One Night Shift	Amy Andrews
Tamed by Her Army Doc's Touch	Lucy Ryder
A Child to Bind Them	Lucy Clark
The Baby That Changed Her Life	Louisa Heaton

0615 GEN STD LP

MILLS & BOON®
Hardback – August 2015

ROMANCE

The Greek Demands His Heir	Lynne Graham
The Sinner's Marriage Redemption	Annie West
His Sicilian Cinderella	Carol Marinelli
Captivated by the Greek	Julia James
The Perfect Cazorla Wife	Michelle Smart
Claimed for His Duty	Tara Pammi
The Marakaios Baby	Kate Hewitt
Billionaire's Ultimate Acquisition	Melanie Milburne
Return of the Italian Tycoon	Jennifer Faye
His Unforgettable Fiancée	Teresa Carpenter
Hired by the Brooding Billionaire	Kandy Shepherd
A Will, a Wish...a Proposal	Jessica Gilmore
Hot Doc from Her Past	Tina Beckett
Surgeons, Rivals...Lovers	Amalie Berlin
Best Friend to Perfect Bride	Jennifer Taylor
Resisting Her Rebel Doc	Joanna Neil
A Baby to Bind Them	Susanne Hampton
Doctor...to Duchess?	Annie O'Neil
Second Chance with the Billionaire	Janice Maynard
Having Her Boss's Baby	Maureen Child

MILLS & BOON®
Large Print – August 2015

ROMANCE

The Billionaire's Bridal Bargain	Lynne Graham
At the Brazilian's Command	Susan Stephens
Carrying the Greek's Heir	Sharon Kendrick
The Sheikh's Princess Bride	Annie West
His Diamond of Convenience	Maisey Yates
Olivero's Outrageous Proposal	Kate Walker
The Italian's Deal for I Do	Jennifer Hayward
The Millionaire and the Maid	Michelle Douglas
Expecting the Earl's Baby	Jessica Gilmore
Best Man for the Bridesmaid	Jennifer Faye
It Started at a Wedding...	Kate Hardy

HISTORICAL

A Ring from a Marquess	Christine Merrill
Bound by Duty	Diane Gaston
From Wallflower to Countess	Janice Preston
Stolen by the Highlander	Terri Brisbin
Enslaved by the Viking	Harper St. George

MEDICAL

A Date with Her Valentine Doc	Melanie Milburne
It Happened in Paris...	Robin Gianna
The Sheikh Doctor's Bride	Meredith Webber
Temptation in Paradise	Joanna Neil
A Baby to Heal Their Hearts	Kate Hardy
The Surgeon's Baby Secret	Amber McKenzie

0715 GEN STD LP

MILLS & BOON®

Why shop at millsandboon.co.uk?

Each year, thousands of romance readers find their perfect read at millsandboon.co.uk. That's because we're passionate about bringing you the very best romantic fiction. Here are some of the advantages of shopping at www.millsandboon.co.uk:

* **Get new books first**—you'll be able to buy your favourite books one month before they hit the shops

* **Get exclusive discounts**—you'll also be able to buy our specially created monthly collections, with up to 50% off the RRP

* **Find your favourite authors**—latest news, interviews and new releases for all your favourite authors and series on our website, plus ideas for what to try next

* **Join in**—once you've bought your favourite books, don't forget to register with us to rate, review and join in the discussions

Visit **www.millsandboon.co.uk**
for all this and more today!